They came from two different worlds then. . .

"Serena, I'm sorry. It's obvious I've misjudged you. Forgive me."

She looked into his eyes and saw repentance there, but that did not take away the hurt that somewhere in his mind he doubted her sincerity. Oh, he could apologize, but the thought was there, and she realized she could never live up to his image of what a Christian woman should be. He saw her only as someone desirous of pleasing herself, a self-centered star used to getting her own way, a woman clever at bringing attention to herself.

"Serena," he said gently, taking her hand, "let's talk about this some more."

She swallowed, near tears. This man had spoiled a lovely dream, for the church and for them as a couple.

"Another time, perhaps. I really must go."

She pulled her hand from his and was out the door but then turned around. "I hope you enjoy Mary Upton's pie!" She threw the words at him, then hurried to the car even though he called her name over and over.

W9-AOA-839

KATHLEEN YAPP lives in Georgia with her husband; they have four children and six grandchildren. She is an accomplished writer of both contemporary and historical romances. Her works include *Romance at Redhaven* and *Speak Softly, Love.*

Don't miss out on any of our super romances. Write to us at the following address for information on our newest releases and club information.

Heartsong Presents Reader's Service
P.O. Box 719
Uhrichsville, OH 44683

A New
Song

Kathleen Yapp

Heartsong Presents

*To my father, Lawerence Peterson, 1898-1979,
who was a faithful minister of the Gospel for forty-
five years. He gave me a most wonderful life, in
and away from church, because he showed the
perfect love of Jesus Christ in all that he did. He
always had time for me.*

*My most vivid memory of him is at his desk,
studying the Scriptures.*

Unless otherwise noted, all scripture quotations are from the
New King James version of the Bible, ©1979, 1980, 1982,
1984 by Thomas Nelson, Inc., Nashville Tennessee and are
used by permission.

ISBN 1-55748-474-0

A NEW SONG

Copyright © 1994 by Kathleen Yapp. All rights reserved.
Except for use in any review, the reproduction or utilization of
this work in whole or in part in any form by any electronic,
mechanical, or other means, now known or hereafter
invented, is forbidden without the permission of the publisher,
Heartsong Presents, P.O. Box 719, Uhrichsville, Ohio 44683

All of the characters and events in this book are fictitious.
Any resemblance to actual persons, living or dead, or to
actual events is purely coincidental.

PRINTED IN THE U.S.A.

one

She was the most beautiful woman he had ever seen—and she sang with a voice only God could have given.

If Steve Shepherd were the kind of man who believed in love at first sight, he would think he had fallen in love with Serena Lawrence. How foolish, though, to think love could hit him like that, sitting here in the Woodruff Arts Center in midtown Atlanta, listening to this glamorous, sophisticated opera star singing with the Atlanta Symphony Orchestra.

He'd seen her on television in *Aida* and *The Magic Flute*, and had listened to her on CDs and records, but the mere beauty of her voice had not prepared him for the magnetism of her personality as it touched him in his fourth-row seat. She seemed to sing for him, and him alone. She had beauty and presence, intelligence and mystery, all blended into one exquisite woman who took his breath away. He was very much afraid she had captured his heart.

It's her talent I admire, he told himself, *nothing more*. But despite the cool logic of his thoughts, he couldn't ignore how lovely she was—small, curvaceous, wearing a shimmering floor-length gown of satin, in his favorite jade green. Her thick auburn hair, pulled straight back in a massive chignon at the back of her head, gave her a regal appearance that was enhanced by the graceful way her hands moved as she sang in French or German or Italian or English. *She has to be a Christian*, Steve thought. *There's a special love inside of her. I know it.*

The sold-out audience of 1700 was as mesmerized as he. No one stirred, or coughed. They just stared and listened—to musical perfection.

Her program was rigorous, including not only operatic arias and classical masterpieces, but spirituals and several numbers from current Broadway hits. When at last she had finished, the audience gave Serena Lawrence a standing ovation and called her back to the stage for two encores.

Steve stood with everyone else, and applauded till his hands hurt. He was glad he had a reason to meet her backstage, and his nerves thrilled with an uncommon excitement.

He was there, in Symphony Hall, with two other members of the Graylin Arts Council. Graylin, a town of 18,000 in northeast Georgia, may have been small, but its representatives had big plans for it. They had come to Atlanta with the absurd hope that Serena Lawrence would come to Graylin and give a concert to help raise money for a new performing arts center.

He had not been the one who had thought of asking her. In fact, when the idea had first surfaced, he'd laughed, thinking it impossible that so busy a celebrity would take time to perform in an obscure town when she was used to singing in the great cities of the world.

Amazingly, though, Miss Lawrence had agreed to see them after the concert, to discuss the matter. Steve could not remember the last time he had been so anxious to meet someone.

"Close your mouth, Stephen, you're gawking like a schoolboy."

The admonition was given, along with a gentle nudge, by an elegant white-haired lady in her seventies who stood on his right. Vivian Barnsley Hall, the executive director of the Arts Council, looked up at his six-foot-two-inch height from her own five feet and three inches with an expression that indicated she expected to be heeded. He smiled. Miss Vivian was the quintessential Southern woman who never raised her voice but was instantly obeyed by all. He obeyed, too, and closed his mouth.

"You'd think you'd never seen a woman before," she added, looking straight ahead at the stage and continuing her gentle applause that barely made a noise.

"I've never seen a woman like her." Steve's voice was low enough that only Miss Vivian could hear.

She sighed. "I do hope you're not going to embarrass us when we meet Miss Lawrence. Try to act like the successful and respected man you are, and not like someone who has never been exposed to the finer things of life."

"Yes, Ma'am," Steve replied, chuckling. His mother had used very similar words when she'd taught him manners when he was a boy. "I'll make you proud of me. Promise."

"Good."

Years of experience enabled Serena Lawrence after each song to smile and nod to the cheering crowd. She was always the consummate professional, graciously accepting accolades even as her heart pounded its denial against the wall of her chest.

The audience made it clear her performance was all they had expected from her, but for Serena, singing tonight was like dancing on the precipice of disaster. Any second she could fail.

The first twenty minutes had been fine. Her aria, "Un bel dì" from *Butterfly*, was flawless, until the final B-flat when she felt the weakness, the rawness at the back of the throat, as though she would lose control of the note at any second. After that, coming upon her without warning, she had . . . episodes, when she had had trouble holding a pitch, or keeping a passage strong.

Now she was struggling to get through the nightmarish performance to the very end, without incident, praying all the while that no one else was noticing. The strain of not knowing when this "weakness" would strike was taking its toll on her emotionally and physically.

Mentally, she forced herself on. Two songs to go. One. Then it was over. A miracle of God had gotten her through the entire program, even the two encores.

But her throat roared in pain. What was the matter with her?

It was her own fault, of course. Dr. Jeffries had warned her not to sing again. He had firmly told her, "You absolutely must rest your throat, Serena, and we must take a biopsy of your vocal cords. To be sure."

To be sure she did not have—cancer.

Her legs trembling so much she feared she would collapse, Serena swept offstage, whispering a prayer under her breath, "Thank you, dear Lord, for getting me through." Along the route to her dressing room, she felt hands reach out to her and voices say, "Magnificent performance, Miss Lawrence. . . . Thrilling. . . . I wept when you sang. . . ."

She smiled and murmured thanks for their compliments, but with her eyes fixed ahead, she saw only a blur of faces. She walked rapidly, focused on getting to the security of the room, inside, away from everyone, where she could release the terror that had gripped her for over an hour.

When she reached the door at last, she could barely manage to turn the doorknob, her hand was trembling so much. Once inside, she whipped the door shut behind her and fell back against it for support, her breathing labored now that she was free to release the performance's fear and pain. A gasp of anguish rushed from her mouth and she closed her eyes tight, wanting a world of darkness instead of reality.

I could have ruined my career, she agonized, disgusted with herself for not having listened to her doctor. She had paid the throat specialist a fortune for his advice, advice she had then ignored.

She had told herself she was keeping her engagement with the Atlanta Symphony because living up to a contract was the conscientious thing to do, but she realized now she was here only because of her stubborn pride. She knew now how foolish she had been.

What if I've made it worse? What if now it's irreparable? She groaned softly and hugged herself. "What if I never sing again?" she whispered out loud, giving words to her greatest fear.

She staggered across the room, taking deep gulps of air, and sank down at her dressing table. With shaking hands, she poured herself a glass of water from a small crystal pitcher. Her eyes drifted up to the mirror in front of her, and she gazed long at the classic face staring back at her, at the three thousand dollar gown, at the diamond necklace and matching earrings.

"I have it all," she said to her image, "fame, fortune, prestige." She swallowed hard. "Tomorrow, I may have nothing." Her eyes flooded with tears, but a sharp knock on the door caused her to fight back the emotion that had almost overwhelmed her.

Deborah, her dresser and companion, opened the door. "You never sounded better," assured the woman in her late forties with very red, very short hair. "The reviews will be great. Atlanta has always adored you."

She patted Serena on the back, then moved through the

room straightening up clothes and magazines and whisking out of sight bone china cups half filled with cold coffee.

"Thank you," Serena answered absently over her shoulder as she struggled to regain her composure. Not even this feisty, caring woman, her friend who traveled with her everywhere, knew her awful secret.

"The people from Graylin will be here any minute," Deborah said, closing a book on the coffee table.

Serena frowned. "Who?"

"From the Arts Council. They want you to sing in their town."

"Oh. . .yes." Concern raced through Serena. How could she meet anyone now?

"Why you ever agreed to talk with them is beyond me," Deborah grumbled. "When would you ever have time to put on a concert in such an unheard-of place? You're scheduled to record a new album in three weeks, and after that you're on tour in Europe, and then in October there's *Madam Butterfly* at the London Opera House, Covent Gardens. You never rest. Have you ever even heard of this Graylin?"

Serena willed herself to relax. Sometimes Deborah's rantings were tedious, but mostly they were entertaining, not to mention wise. "Have you?" she questioned back.

Deborah snorted, "If it has less than five hundred thousand people, it's not on my map. Or yours either."

She stopped her fussing and gazed thoughtfully at Serena, as though sensing that something was not right with her. "You're not seriously thinking of going there, are you?"

Serena sighed and stared again at the image of herself in the mirror. "I don't know, really, but some small voice in my head is telling me I should."

A polite knock on the door sent Deborah scurrying to open it, and three people entered the room, two women and a man. Serena's eyes settled on each of the women in turn as she graciously shook their hands and learned their names. However, when she put her still-trembling hand into the large, warm one of the tall, very handsome man with sandy blond hair, her breath stopped.

"Steve Shepherd," he introduced himself in a rich baritone voice. Serena gazed up into soft brown eyes that danced with life and interest.

He was more than good-looking, with a long, straight nose and a strong, well-shaped mouth that was smiling, making two dimples crease his cheeks. His eyes, though, were what mesmerized her. They were the kindest eyes she'd ever seen, as though he knew all her secrets and still admired her. Something about him made her calm and excited at the same time.

"Hello," she said softly, knowing in that instant he was someone special.

two

"You were marvelous tonight. Really superb," Steve said. He held her gaze with his, awed that she was even more beautiful close up where he could see the delicate curve of her mouth and the luxurious fringe of lashes that surrounded her large, expressive eyes.

"Thank you."

"I'm a great fan of yours."

"Oh?"

He grinned. "Well, I haven't started a fan club yet or compiled a scrapbook," they both chuckled, "but I think I have every CD you've recorded and a couple of operas on video tape."

He watched, in amazement, as she blushed.

"I'm grateful you like my music," she said.

"I do." *And I like you, too*, Steve could have added, but caught himself just before he did. After all, he'd promised Miss Vivian he wouldn't embarrass them by acting like a lovestruck teenager.

But keeping that promise might not be easy. Not when he stood close enough to Serena Lawrence to smell the woodsy-scent of her perfume, to see the curve of her throat, the flawless skin of her oval face, the sweep of full eyebrows. . . .

"Thank you for seeing us, Miss Lawrence," he heard Miss Vivian say. He caught his associate's frown over the diva's shoulder, and realized he was still holding Serena's hand. He quickly dropped it, while Miss Vivian continued, "We know you are exhausted from your performance, so we shall only say that we hope you will consider coming to our lovely town to help us raise money for a much-needed performing arts center."

Miss Lawrence turned her attention to the two women, and Steve took a long, slow breath. He realized his pulse was racing, and he needed all his concentration to bring his mind back to the reason they were there.

"The Graylin Arts Council is made up of twenty-four arts organizations in the area," the other member of the council, Mrs. Oliver, said. She was an attractive, energetic woman in her late forties who worked diligently for a half dozen worthy committees in their town. "There's Brandon University, the Graylin Symphony Orchestra and Ballet Company, Hall County Museum, the Quade Art Center, Elachee Nature Science Center, Graylin Theatre Alliance. . . ."

Her recital went on while Steve's mind refocused on Serena Lawrence. She was stunningly beautiful, and gracious, and soft-spoken (*Is she Southern?* he wondered), and nice. So very, very nice. And genuine. Her attitude toward them held no condescension, no haughty pride.

She was like a piece of exquisite porcelain that no man could help but admire—and yet he had read recently that she was not married. Steve wondered why, as his eyes fell on a magnificent arrangement of yellow roses in a crystal vase. Was whoever sent them important to her?

"Don't you agree, Stephen?"

He heard the words, with just the slightest edge of irritation to them, and knew he was in trouble. Miss Vivian was speaking to him, in her perfectly modulated voice with its smooth and unhurried pronunciation, and he hadn't the foggiest notion what she'd said. From the upturn of her well-defined eyebrows, she was expecting an answer, so he flashed her a big smile and said enthusiastically, "Of course I agree."

"Excellent," she responded.

Serena Lawrence looked up at him, the color of her questioning eyes exactly the same green as her dress, and said, "Are you sure you'll have time?"

Time for what? he thought in panic.

"I'm sure you're a busy man. I wouldn't want to be an imposition," she went on.

He gaped at her. "You could never be that, Miss Lawrence."

"Stephen Shepherd has lived in Graylin most of his life," Mrs. Oliver said. "He knows its history and its present. If anyone can introduce you to the character of our precious town, it is he. You couldn't ask for a better guide."

"Or someone more able to explain the workings of the Arts Council," Miss Vivian added.

The three women all turned to Steve, eyeing him as though he were the next best thing to dessert. He, on the other hand, felt like he'd just been hit by an avalanche. *Guide? As in show Miss Lawrence around Graylin?* He, alone, with her? Was she actually agreeing to come to their town?

"I would very much like to learn more about the Council before I make up my mind about doing a concert," Miss Lawrence said to him, her pink-tinged lips separating to expose perfectly white teeth, "and touring the city while learning about the Council's supporters would help me make a decision."

Is everything about her flawless? Steve knew of course that outward beauty was not the sum total of a woman's value, but it certainly had the power to attract.

"I need a little. . .vacation," she continued, "and your Graylin sounds the perfect place."

"It's quiet compared with the cities you're used to," Steve managed to say.

"That's why the idea appeals to me. But are you sure you're not too busy—"

"No, no, not at all. I'd love to be with you—uh, spend

time with you—show you around. . . ." He threw a desperate look at Vivian who glared at him over the top of her glasses. Apparently, she was prepared to leave him out on the limb all alone.

"I would be honored, Miss Lawrence," Miss Vivian finally rescued him, "if you would stay with me while you are in Graylin. My home will be at your disposal for as long as you choose. The members of the Arts Council know what a tremendous favor we are asking of you, to give a concert in our small community, but," and she lavished on the opera diva a smile that few people could have resisted, "we wanted at least to ask."

Serena nodded her head. "I'm happy you did. It may be that fate has brought us together for mutual good."

"Or God," Steve said.

Serena froze in place and Steve caught his breath. He hadn't meant to correct her. When her gaze settled on him, he was glad to see she was not angry, just thoughtful.

"Do you believe in God, Mr. Shepherd?"

"Oh, yes," he assured her.

"So do I, in which case, you may be right that God has brought us together."

"We would leave the choice of date for the concert entirely up to you," Mrs. Oliver suggested enthusiastically. "We were thinking the beginning of fall would be good, but if you would rather do it sooner, that would be marvelous, too. All the Arts Council members will work very hard to do whatever is necessary to make the venture a success."

"I'm sure you will," Serena said.

"We've taken up far more of your time than we should have, Miss Lawrence," Vivian declared, "so we'll let Stephen and you make arrangements." She turned to Steve. "Mrs. Oliver and I will meet you out in the lobby."

"Fine," he agreed.

The women left, and the other woman, whom Steve concluded worked for Miss Lawrence, went about some chores on the other side of the room.

He knew he should be saying something. He needed to let Miss Lawrence get on with the business of winding down from the emotional evening, but although he was a man who made his living by speaking, he found himself tongue-tied. His reaction to her puzzled him, for he was not a man to make quick judgments of people, either good or bad. Still, he could not deny that he relished the thought of spending time with her—and it wasn't just for the sake of the Arts Council—but his feelings surprised him.

He had been lonely for so long. Not since his wife had died of leukemia years before had he been involved with a woman. Well-meaning friends were always trying to find "the perfect woman" for him. They urged him to go out, get married again, but he had never been interested. His heart was bruised in more ways than even his closest friends knew, and he had not met anyone yet who could heal the wound.

Of course, he had prayed to the Lord about his marriage with Stacia, before and during their few years together. As the problems grew, so did his trust in God to help him work things out. Even in the midst of his marriage's worst turbulence, he had experienced God's peace.

When Stacia died, though, he had been devastated. He knew she had not been happy with him or their life together, and he felt guilty that the stress of their relationship had possibly contributed to her illness. Many times he wondered why God had allowed Stacia to die.

No, it would be a miracle for him to feel love for a woman again. In fact, he had felt nothing for any of the ones he had met recently—until now. Until Serena Lawrence, who was the most unlikely person in the entire world to appeal to him. *Why her, Lord?* he was questioning now as they stood gazing at each other.

"I enjoyed this evening very much," he said in a low voice, the timbre of which thrilled Serena. She had always preferred the bass register for a man, and this Stephen Shepherd was definitely a man—tall, lanky, with well-groomed hair that just begged to have a woman's fingers running through it. His face was smoothly handsome, accented by those adorable dimples.

"Thank you for saying so," she answered him, aware of a fluttery feeling meandering through her.

"Do you prefer concerts to operas?" he asked.

"It doesn't matter, as long as I'm singing. I sing while I'm driving, and while I'm cooking, and maybe even in my sleep."

Steve's laugh was a soft rumble, and Serena liked it, too, just as she did everything else about him so far. "I could come tomorrow to Graylin," she said impulsively, "if you could pick me up at my hotel. I'm staying at the Ritz-Carlton on Peachtree Road."

Steve grinned. "An excellent hotel. What time?"

"As early in the morning as you can make it."

His slightly shaggy eyebrows raised. "After tonight won't you be sleeping late?"

Serena laughed gaily. "No. I much prefer getting up early. Mornings are my most productive time. If I get tired during the day, I take a nap. What about you? Are you a morning person, too, Mr. Shepherd?"

"Please call me Steve," he urged.

Serena gazed into his eyes a moment longer than she should have and answered softly, "All right. . .Steve, if you'll call me Serena."

The short silence between them was electric. At last he said, "I'm not sure if I'm a morning person or not. And as to naps, I don't take enough of them to know whether I like them or not."

"Oh, they're wonderful. They revitalize you for the rest of the day and evening."

"I imagine that in your world you need a lot of energy at all times of the day and night."

"Yes, that's true."

They hung on each other's every word, and yet their words hardly mattered, as anyone else listening to them would have recognized. Lost in each other's presence, what they were saying was not what mattered. The important thing was the sense of discovery they each felt, as though their words revealed their hearts.

"I do meet myself coming and going sometimes," Serena went on, "I haven't learned the knack of slowing down. But I really must take a few days off and rest. Doctor's orders."

Steve frowned. "You've been to a doctor?"

Serena silently berated her carelessness. "He's a dear friend of the family who's always telling me I do too much. So this time, I'm going to please him, and follow his advice."

"Vacations can be fun," Steve said, remembering the many happy ones he had shared with his parents, but feeling hypocritical because he seldom took one these days.

Serena felt a surge of excitement. "Will I have a good time in Graylin, Steve?"

"I hope so. Small towns have a lot more going on in them than most people think."

"And is Graylin charming?"

"That, and more," he promised her.

"I shall look forward to seeing it, then."

"And I in showing it to you. How about ten tomorrow morning?"

"Perfect."

She extended her hand. He took it in his and held it. "Wear comfortable clothes," he suggested. "After we get you settled with Miss Vivian, there's something special I want to show you."

"All right." Serena sighed in delight. A thoughtful, enterprising man. Just what she needed at the moment to distract her from dark thoughts of the future. "It sounds like an adventure awaits us," she said.

Steve nodded. "My mother always used to say, 'Off to adventure,' when we'd start a fun day."

"Then it's off to adventure for us. At ten o'clock tomorrow."

"Yes."

Deborah looked across the room at the two of them, standing close, holding hands, not shaking hands. *She likes him,* she concluded, frowning. *I hope she lets me go with her to this Graylin. I have a feeling she's going to need looking after.*

Steve silently kissed Serena's hand, and Serena's heart tap-danced, something that had not happened to her for a very long time.

"Off to adventure," they both said at the same time, and then they laughed.

three

"Are you comfortable?" Steve asked.

Serena smiled and murmured, "Yes." She relaxed into the passenger seat of the four-door sedan and looked out the window at some of the prettiest country she had ever seen.

As soon as they veered onto I-985, Serena knew she had made the right decision to go to Graylin. The two double lanes of the freeway were separated by a wide corridor of thick, green grass. On the other side of the freeway was an endless expanse of tall pines, delicate dogwoods, and gnarled oaks that blocked out any signs of human existence.

She felt as though the world beyond the two of them in that car had ceased to exist, and for the moment, Serena forgot the horrendous physical problem that had lain so heavily on her mind for months. Here, in the north Georgia countryside, the sun was shining, the sky was brilliant blue, and the man beside her was decidedly handsome.

He wore khaki cotton twill slacks and a matching short sleeved shirt that displayed a long, lithe body, strong but not muscle-bound. The breeze from his open window blew his light blond hair across his broad forehead, and his mouth was relaxed in a half-smile as he concentrated on the road ahead.

Serena was amazed at how comfortable she felt with him. He was practically a stranger, and yet she knew from the group he represented that he was no doubt a music lover; that alone gave them something in common already.

She grew more excited by the moment at the thought of the carefree days ahead of her, grateful to Miss Vivian for offering her the use of her home. For the first time in a long while, Serena would be alone, for Deborah had been persuaded to take some time off. As much as Serena loved Deborah, she knew right now she needed her independence.

"How long will it take us to get there?" she asked Steve with the excitement of an eager child. She noted with admiration the strength of his hands on the steering wheel and the firm set of his jaw as he concentrated on driving.

"From here about thirty minutes." He glanced over at her with a smile. "After we get you settled at Miss Vivian's, I thought I'd drive you by some of the member organizations of the Arts Council—not to go in and talk with them, but just to see where they are located. At the same time, that will give you a good first glimpse of Graylin."

Serena sighed. She liked decisive people. "That sounds perfect. Don't forget about that special place you promised to show me."

He chuckled. "I won't. By the way, tomorrow night the Graylin Chorale will be performing Johannes Brahms' `Requiem' at the First United Methodist Church, if you'd like to hear them. They performed it last year at Carnegie Hall and were well received."

Serena's eyes brightened. "Yes, I'd very much like to do that. How many are in the group?"

"About sixty of our finest vocalists."

"It's a date then," she said enthusiastically, but then realized the implication of her remark and tried to backtrack, "well, not a date, of course. . . ."

Steve nodded his head. "I understand. Actually it will be a good time for you to meet some of the members of the Council, and talk with them, if you like. I know Miss Vivian is going."

Serena relaxed. He hadn't taken her comment as a wish on her part to be more than just friendly acquaintances. Their being together had only to do with a professional situation. Nothing more.

The rolling green hills they were traveling through eventually gave way to the businesses and homes of Graylin. Serena gasped when they turned off the freeway at Exit 5 onto Kings Hill Parkway; the narrow median that separated the two sides of the street was filled with a lavish display of wild flowers.

"How absolutely gorgeous," she cried, revelling in the sight of purple coneflowers, blackeyed susans, Queen Anne's lace, primrose, and several other flowers whose names she did not know.

"It's a project of the Georgia Department of Transportation," Steve explained. "They urge garden clubs and local governments to turn state roads and interstates into wild flower gardens." He slowed the car so that Serena would have longer to enjoy the kaleidoscopic view that stretched block after block.

Yes, he thought to himself, *the flowers are beautiful, but no more beautiful than you, Serena Lawrence.* She was wearing a sleeveless white cotton sundress trimmed with lace; the skirt cinched her small waist beneath a fabric belt, then fell to her calves. Her vibrant auburn hair was loose and hung down to her shoulders, and Steve was sure he had never seen a more gorgeous mane of hair in his life.

The drive from Atlanta had relaxed him, as the open country always did. After the stress of his work, he needed that relaxation. He rarely took a day off, because there was just so much to do. Because of that, this "duty" he'd been given—to present his town to Serena—was certainly not something to which he would have agreed voluntarily. Not because he wouldn't have wanted to be with her, but because of the time involved, time needed for other things.

Since the "duty" had been thrust upon him, however, and he was, after all, an active member of the Arts Council Board of Directors, he felt he could enjoy its benefits without feeling too guilty. He could hardly have said no.

Serena was laughing lightly. "These flowers look so natural, don't they, Steve? As though they had just been blown there and took root of themselves?"

"Sure do."

"But I'm sure there were endless hours of work on the part of a lot of people to plow, till, fertilize the ground, plant the seeds, kill the weeds. . . ." She stopped, embarrassed, and glanced at Steve. "I do tend to get excited about some things."

"Would that everyone loved life the way you do, Serena."

The stricken look on her face made him wonder if he'd said something wrong, especially when she turned in her seat and looked out the window.

A few more blocks went by and he heard her gasp. "Oh, look at those magnificent Victorian homes, all white and grand with their pillars and long, graceful lawns."

"They're called the `Lovely Ladies' by the locals," Steve told her, and Serena murmured her appreciation of the unique, old homes on both sides of the street.

"Each one is different from the others," she exclaimed. "Look, Steve, one of them is a bed-and-breakfast inn. That one is a law firm, and there's a restaurant. Isn't it quaint?"

She turned back to him. "May I buy you lunch at that restaurant for all your trouble in bringing me here?"

"That really isn't necessary—"

"Oh, but I want to," she hurried on, excited over what she was seeing on Dean Street. "Then could we walk along this street? I've never seen so many beautiful old homes all together."

She craned her neck from one direction to another, and Steve knew he could not say no to her, for she had an infectious delight in everything around her.

"I know you're thinking of saying no to lunch," she said, seeming to read his thoughts, "but we have to eat, and after we take my things to Miss Vivian's, we'll both be famished. You know we will. Perhaps Miss Vivian would like to join us."

Steve had no trouble agreeing. He found he wanted to please her, for she was not at all jaded from the sophisticated, well-traveled life she led because of her successful career. Instead, her childlike appreciation of lovely things was endearing. Even though Steve had a dozen other projects he needed to attend to that afternoon, he decided the world would not spin out of control if he took time to have lunch with Serena Lawrence and walk with her along Dean Street. After all, he had an obligation to the Council.

He smiled and turned the car toward Miss Vivian's, wondering if Serena would show equal enthusiasm when she learned what he did for a living. Some people were respectful, while others lost their ability to communicate freely.

He and Serena had talked easily together on the ride from Atlanta—about the weather, music, world news, and the State of Georgia. Serena had told him where she'd been educated, and had just asked him what kind of work he did, when they'd come upon the wild flowers.

He was sure, though, it would come up at lunch, and that was okay, for the sooner she learned he was a minister, the sooner he would learn where she stood spiritually.

"What a charming home you have, Miss Vivian," Serena complimented as she walked through the old but well-kept home on Dirksen Street. It was a one-story, seventy years old, with three large bedrooms, a formal dining room off the kitchen, a great room, and a cozy library.

Except for the wood-paneled library, all the walls were painted pale green, dotted here and there with original oil paintings and some prints. The pictures, by various Georgia artists, depicted life in this Southern state, both in history and currently—laborers picking cotton, a Cherokee Indian overlooking a lush green valley, a magnificent plantation home surrounded by tall magnolias, boaters on the Chattahoochee River, the skyline of Atlanta surrounded by storm clouds.

Most of the furniture was mahogany or cherry wood, and tabletops held various family pictures and memorabilia and antiques that Vivian had inherited from both her side of the family and her husband's. Serena noticed the smallest detail and commented on it, picking up this and that, asking questions about it, enjoying the home that, while simple rather than elegant, was interesting and unique.

"I've lived here a long time," Miss Vivian responded, pleased with her important guest's compliments, "so it's comfortable, though I suspect also cluttered. That's the trouble with being old—one has had decades to collect what one thinks is necessary to keep and never throw away."

Serena carefully stroked a Victorian cranberry epergne filled with fresh yellow daffodils. "I have a very nice apartment in New York," she said, "but I'm seldom there, and most of my furnishings came from a decorator's salon, not from my own family. How fortunate that you've kept so many precious reminders of the people you came from and loved." She sighed wistfully. "We live in a throw-away society, don't we, and only discover when we're more mature that those things we didn't want to be bothered with when we were young are the very things we wish we had kept and treasured?"

Miss Vivian glanced at Steve; each knew they shared the common thought that this young woman was exceptionally sensitive and thoughtful. The sophistication of her life had not dulled her appreciation of what others thought important. Steve was glad for the happiness in Vivian's eyes. She was a special woman and deserved to be appreciated.

Outside, on the quarter-acre of land, Serena exclaimed over the spring garden awash with pink and white azaleas. Red and yellow tulips bordered a brick walk, and a small gazebo nestled under a tall, old weeping willow. When Serena stepped up onto the wooden floor, she whirled around and fixed Steve and Vivian with such a look of joy, they both stopped where they were, entranced. "I will love this place," she declared. "It's perfect for reading or writing to friends or recording in one's diary."

Her eyes sparkled, and Steve's heart lurched for several beats, while his eyes drank in the flush on Serena's cheek and the softness of her hair as it lifted around her face in the breeze.

No wonder she is so able to captivate an audience, he thought, *for she herself is captivating, and full of life.*

He was smitten.

four

Miss Vivian watched Stephen's expression; reading his heart, she did not know whether to be glad or sad. She loved this man and wanted all of life's best for him.

She knew something of the troubled marriage that had ended in the death of his young wife. She sensed the scars he still bore, and she had always feared he would never open his heart to love again.

And yet she was watching it happen now—but how could Serena Lawrence be the right woman? Their careers locked them into different worlds: hers the constantly moving world of the professional singer and his this small town. Both their works demanded their full attention; they could never have time for each other.

Her eyes shifted to Serena, a young woman who had achieved stardom, yet was able to enjoy the simple pleasure of a spring afternoon. If she were an ordinary woman, one who lived here, who wanted a husband and children, who could love someone in Stephen's profession...ah, but that could never be. She belonged to others.

Serena smiled at Vivian and Steve. "Why do I feel so comfortable with you both? And this house?" Her slender arms gestured all around her. "And this town?"

Steve cleared his throat, wondering if he would ever be in her presence without feeling enchanted. "Are you ready for lunch?" he asked, having already put her suitcases in the pretty bedroom Vivian had chosen for her.

"Yes, I'm starved," she answered. "Will you join us, Miss Vivian? Steve is going to take me to Victor's on Dean Street, and afterward, we're going to walk by those beautiful old

27

homes, and then drive by some of the member organizations of the Arts Council and see a little of Graylin."

Vivian smiled at them both. "It sounds delightful, but this is my afternoon for volunteer work at the hospital. Stephen," she turned to him, "why don't we take Serena to the Chorale concert tomorrow night?"

"I already mentioned it to her, Miss Vivian, and she wants to go."

"Yes, I do, very much," Serena confirmed.

"Splendid, then we can go together, and I shall introduce you to other members of the Council Board who will be there."

Stephen and Serena left for their drive, and Vivian watched them walk away: vibrant, handsome young people, both brilliant at what they did, both respected and admired by countless others. Stephen was happy, but lonely—though he would never admit it. Serena, she had learned—for she was a great fan of hers and knew much of her life story—had never married and had no children. Was she as happy as she seemed?

Vivian heard the car doors shut, and she wondered if she had been right to urge Stephen to become a member of the Arts Council. He certainly had enough to do without that involvement, she well knew, but she had thought it would be good for him to be in a different environment than the one he faced every day. She was sure he enjoyed his service to the community, and probably was telling himself at that very moment that his squiring Serena Lawrence about town was all in the line of duty.

But Vivian had seen the interest in his eyes, the smile of appreciation as he watched Serena. *Oh, Stephen,* she thought fearfully, *have I put temptation in your path?*

Serena lost all track of time as they drove around Graylin. Steve showed her many of the companies and organizations that supported the Arts Council, and she saw a city that was charming in places and ugly in others. Some streets were wide and modern, others narrow and picturesque, still others depressing. Prestigious neighborhoods and elegant subdivisions stood in stark contrast to the dilapidated, unpainted houses or trailers of the poor and less fortunate.

Almost everywhere, though, flowers grew.

The downtown streets had no parking meters, and the one-story banks looked more like houses than places of business. Some buildings were new; others old and unkempt.

All in all it was a town of personality, belonging to both the rich and the poor, to whites, blacks, and Hispanics. Quaint local restaurants, specializing in barbecue pork, chicken and biscuits, or all the catfish one could eat, rubb.. shoulders with the usual McDonald's, Wendy's and Arby's.

"I can't get over how far the houses are set back from the road, and the distance between them," Serena said as they traveled south along Poplar Street out of the city. "I'm used to skyscrapers and cement and only patches where the sun gets through. Just look at the beautiful lawns and the spring flowers. The dogwoods are gorgeous. Oh, there's a pink one."

When they reached the country, she was equally as excited about the rolling fields of grass, the black cows grazing contentedly, and the ducks she saw waddling beside a pond. "Did you see that horse look at us when we drove by?" she asked Steve, and when he chuckled, she turned to him and said with a frown, "Why are you laughing at me?"

He shook his head. "I'm appreciating your *joie de vivre*."

"My joy of life?"

"Yes. There's no doubting you're an artist, because you see and feel the world around you to a degree most of us don't."

"You make me sound naive."

"Not at all." He pulled off the highway, onto a narrow cement road. "You have a gift for making people see things in a new way."

"What people?"

"Me."

He stopped the car. They were in the parking lot of an red brick church, with white trim around the windows and doors, and a tall, white steeple from which carillon bells were chiming "Rock of Ages."

"That's another thing that impresses me about this town," Serena said, "its churches. Is there one on every corner? And do they all have their own cemeteries? I'm sure we've seen half a dozen just on the drive here."

Steve got out and came around to open the car door for her. He stepped back as she got out, but he still caught the scent of her perfume as she brushed by him.

"This is the Bible Belt," he reminded her, "and people here are open about their Christianity."

"Mmm."

She said nothing more but looked at the good-sized church, its adjacent buildings, and then at its cemetery that was neat and awash with flowers at nearly every grave.

"Do you go to church, Steve?" she asked.

He gave her a big grin "Yes, ma'am. This one, in fact."

"Really?"

"Would you like to go inside?"

"May we?"

"Sure."

He stepped ahead of her in order to open the door, and they walked into a foyer that was filled with sunlight and the scent of the fresh flowers that sat on an oak table in the center of the room.

"Oh, this is lovely, Steve."

She went to the huge, round table, and picked up one of the bulletins from the previous Sunday's service; Steve wondered if she would see his name. When she put the bulletin back on the table, he knew she hadn't, although she commented, "This is certainly a flourishing church. There's a lot going on every day."

"Let me show you the sanctuary," he offered. Taking her arm seemed a natural thing to do, and he guided her toward two mammoth oak doors. Inside, Serena only took a few steps along the hunter green carpet before she stopped and sucked in her breath.

The room was octagonal in shape, capable of holding four or five hundred people, she guessed, and slanted downward past sturdy wooden pews covered with plush cushions of the same deep green color as the carpet. Her eyes traveled beyond a curving altar in the front, to a broad carpeted platform that held fine wooden furniture, a gigantic pulpit, a concert grand piano, and an organ whose many pipes soared to the ceiling on either side of a huge cross. The choir loft held enough seats for a fifty-member choir, with a baptismal to one side.

What caught Serena's eye then were the two walls of stained glass windows, depicting six well-known Bible verses. Through them sunlight was streaming, and Serena turned and said, "This is magnificent, Steve. One can feel God in this place."

Steve felt a lump in his throat. That was exactly his reaction every time he entered this room which was, of course, dedicated to the glory of God and His purposes.

Serena laid her hand on the back of a pew. "Are there good people here?"

"Yes," Steve said, "and not-so-good, too."

Serena looked at him in surprise.

"We have a few saints, that's true, but most of us are walking our daily life of faith in varying degrees of victory."

Serena frowned and Steve saw the light go out of her eyes. "It's not always easy to be the kind of Christian one wants to be," she said thoughtfully.

"That's true," he agreed.

She walked slowly toward the front. "When I was growing up, my parents and I went to church twice on Sunday, and every Wednesday as well, for Bible Study. Then there were the activities. Oh, yes, lots and lots of activities for all ages." A sound of bitterness crept into her voice. "Whether you were a toddler or a senior citizen, the church had plenty for you to do. Every time the doors opened, they wanted you there."

She reached the altar, and stood staring down at it, strange emotions tugging at her heart. Sometimes, growing up, she had knelt at just such an altar, the first time at age seven, to ask forgiveness of her sin. After that she had come for various reasons, sometimes for herself, sometimes on behalf of others. She remembered those cries of help to God, and how she had always felt refreshed and comforted after praying at the altar, and she wished she could feel now the confidence she had had as a child that God could solve all her problems.

She had been taught that God could do that. Both her father and mother had believed that, and she had, too, until her mother had died, too young, leaving Serena a crushed, bewildered fourteen-year-old girl whose faith in God was shaken. From then on her fellowship in God's house had diminished, and eventually other things moved in to fill the void.

Now, instead of feeling again the excitement of being in God's house, of being in His will, she felt only the old resentment that He had demanded too much from her mother. He had allowed her to be taken away just when she was needed the most by her family.

Serena turned and saw Steve studying her. She was glad he could not read her mind, for her thoughts were not what they should be in this place.

five

"I'm sure people enjoy worshiping here," Serena said, trying to sound upbeat, trying to chase the hurtful memories from her mind.

Steve was about to answer her when the door behind them burst open, and a short, pudgy man in his early sixties exploded into the room.

"Oh, there you are," he exclaimed, walking as quickly as his short legs would carry him down the aisle toward them. "I thought you would be in your office today," he said to Steve.

"I had business," Steve responded.

The gray mood that had invaded Serena deepened when she heard Steve describe their being together as business. Of course that was what it was, but from the very first moment she'd met him, there had been something more between them—an easy camaraderie, a comfortableness that felt like they were old friends. And there was attraction. She had thought he felt it, too, but maybe not, since he was describing her as "business."

Steve introduced her to the man whose name was Walter Thomas. "Walter is the head of our deacon board," Steve explained.

From the look on Walter's face, Serena could tell he did not know who she was, or what she meant to Steve Shepherd. "I'm happy to meet you," she said.

"Same here." He gave her a half smile, then said to Steve. "There are four people to be baptized a week from this Sunday."

Serena wondered why he was telling Steve this. Was Steve the maintenance man who would fill the baptismal and make ready the dressing rooms?

With a sudden jolt of frustration, she realized she did not know what Steve did for a living. She had asked him once, just before they'd arrived in Graylin, but something had distracted their attention, and he'd never told her.

She was embarrassed. *Steve must think I'm terribly self-centered*, she thought, *only talking of myself, and not having the common courtesy to ask what his work is.*

"Mary Upton will be among them," Mr. Thomas told Steve, and Serena caught a certain look in his eye that seemed to say that this Mary Upton was unique from the others.

"I'm glad Mary is going to be baptized," Steve said, his baritone voice forever pleasing to Serena's ear. "Do you think any of her family will be there?"

"I think so. Even though they're disappointed she's no longer attending the family church on Bryant Street, they're glad she's fellowshipping regularly here," Mr. Thomas stated. "They think highly of you, Steve."

"And I respect the Uptons. They're an old Southern family who has done a lot for this community and state."

"My wife and I have invited Mary to dinner tonight," Walter said. "We'd like you to come, too. It's been a long time since we've had you over."

"Thanks for the invitation, Walter, but I'm afraid I can't tonight."

Steve didn't know whether to laugh or be annoyed at Walter's continuing efforts to find him a wife. This man, who had a happy and solid marriage, wanted the same for every other man, and six months after Steve had become a widower, Walter had started his campaign to find a perfect woman for him.

Only Steve had wanted no part of it, because he still felt tied to Stacia and recognized fully the major problems their relationship had struggled with—lack of time together and little commitment on Stacia's part to her role as pastor's wife. Before he ever got married again, *if* he ever got married again, he knew he would have to learn to better balance his time between church and home, and his wife would have to be sent from God, with a calling to God's work that was as deep as his.

That's the way he had felt then, when Walter had first started bringing this woman and that to his attention, and he still felt the same way. He relished the long hours spent on church work and, though he was lonely for the love of a woman and companionship, he hadn't yet met anyone who had made him think of marrying again. That's why Walter kept trying.

"Mary is a lovely girl, Steve."

"I know."

Steve glanced over at Serena and gave her a smile. He didn't like conversations that left people out, and this one had nothing to do with Serena.

"Did you know she's just taken a position at Everitt Academy?"

"No, I didn't."

"She's teaching English Literature and, I've heard, is doing very well."

"I'm sure the young ladies will appreciate Mary's intelligence."

Walter smiled. "To be capable as well as pretty is not given to all women, but it certainly has been to Mary Upton."

Steve could not believe the blatancy with which Walter was "selling" the latest candidate for pastor's wife.

"Yes, Walter, Mary is both pretty and smart, and I know

I would enjoy getting to know her better at your house, but I really cannot make it tonight."

Walter's expression fell.

"I have other plans." Steve knew his excuse was feeble, and he caught his deacon's glance at Serena. Walter was no doubt surmising that she was the reason his plans were being thwarted.

The silence grew awkward, until at last Walter took a handkerchief out of his pocket and wiped the sweat from his forehead. Stuffing it back in a pocket inside his suit jacket, he said, "Well, I just thought it would be nice for the pastor to get to know better one of his most devoted parishioners. That's all I intended."

I'm sure, Steve thought with a silent chuckle.

Serena stared at Walter. Then her eyes raced to Steve. Had she heard right? Was Steve Shepherd a pastor? Was this man she was beginning to like in a non-professional way a minister? She wanted to scream, *What kind of cruel joke is this? To finally meet a man who interests me in so many ways, only to learn that he is tied to the very institution I haven't been involved with for a long time, nor intend to be again.*

"Excuse me," she said curtly, and walked past Steve and Mr. Thomas up the aisle and out the door, her heart pounding. *It isn't fair*, she thought angrily. *Why does he have to belong to the church?*

Steve felt her distance when she passed him, and was puzzled. Serena had been happy, interested in the church . . .until. . .until what?

"I have to go, Walter," he said, and started after Serena, but Walter stopped him by taking hold of his arm.

"We need to talk about the board's financial report. It's almost ready to show the congregation and I need some input from you. That's another reason I want you to come to dinner."

The financial report was important, and Steve had been wanting to talk with Walter about it before it was released, but now was not the time. His mind wasn't on it. His mind was on a woman he liked more than he should.

"I'm sorry, Walter, I just can't tonight. Come by the office tomorrow."

He was concerned for Serena and wanted to find her. Was she ill? Was she upset about something? Whatever it was, he knew he had to fix it. Wanted to fix it. Wanted her to be smiling again—at him.

He caught up with her in the cemetery. She was meandering amongst the tombstones, looking down at them, twisting her hands at her waist. He didn't need his degree in psychology to know she was troubled about something.

"Serena, what's wrong?"

She continued walking, without looking up at him.

"Are you all right?" he asked.

She paused, getting control of herself, berating her silly display of temper. What difference did it make that Steve Shepherd was a pastor? His responsibility had been to show her around Graylin. That he had done. Now that she was settled at Miss Vivian's, other people could explain to her about the Arts Council and make arrangements for the concert.

Steve Shepherd was just a nice man who had given her a few hours of pleasant company. That was all. That was all there could ever be between them, even though deep in her heart she suspected she was developing feelings for him.

She turned and gave him a weak smile. "I'm fine," she said.

She studied the handsome lines of his face, the warmth in his eyes, the frown of concern that wrinkled his forehead. She liked that face. She liked this man, far more than she should for knowing him such a short time.

The smile disappeared. "Why didn't you tell me you were a minister?" There was an edge to her question that she couldn't help. For too many years she had blamed the church for taking someone from her. Letting go of old resentments was hard, even with someone as nice as Steve Shepherd.

"I wasn't trying to keep my ministry a secret, Serena. It only came up once, when we first arrived in Graylin, but our attention was distracted to the wild flowers and that's why I didn't answer. Why does it upset you?" He searched her eyes for an explanation.

Serena forced a smile to her lips. *It isn't Steve's fault about Mother. He's been so kind to me, and I'm treating him as though he were a leper.*

"Forgive me, please. I have a spiritual wound that has never healed, and every once in awhile it surfaces and causes pain."

Steve frowned more deeply. "Do you want to talk about it?"

Serena shook her head. "It's better left in the past." She shook herself out of her mood and asked brightly, "Is it usual for a minister to be a member of an arts council?"

Steve chuckled. "I admit that I have more than enough to do in this pastorate to fill every day with forty-eight hours instead of just twenty-four," he told her, "but Miss Vivian said I needed an outside interest, that I would get stale if I didn't expose myself to something other than the church."

"Miss Vivian?"

"Yes. She's a member of my church, and has, for years, given herself the unofficial duty of caring for the pastor.

She gives me advice on my health," he began to smile at the memories of Vivian's hovering, "reminds me of the importance of taking vacation days from time to time, supervises my love life—"

"Your love life?"

"I don't have one."

"That's too bad," Serena said, but didn't mean it.

They began to walk along the narrow gravel path, their arms touching sometimes as the path was not wide. Serena found that his closeness relaxed her. Steve pondered what had happened in her past that troubled her so.

"Walter, whom you just met," he said, "is on the same wave length as Vivian: they both think I need another wife."

Serena turned to him. "Another wife?"

"My wife died some years ago, Serena."

"Oh."

"The main reason Walter invited me to dinner tonight is to dangle another candidate under my nose."

"Mary Upton?"

"Yes."

Serena felt a stab of jealousy, and it caught her off guard, making her feel ridiculous. Why should she care what woman was in Steve Shepherd's life? "Do you need a wife?" she asked.

Steve stopped and gazed into the distance, while Serena glimpsed the loneliness that flickered across his features.

"I probably do, but I don't want one," he said.

She was surprised at that remark. "Why don't you?"

"I didn't do very well with the first one I had, and I'm not at all sure there will ever be a second. To be the pastor's wife is not a position most women want when it means sharing your husband with hundreds of other people, never knowing when he'll be home, living with a man who's so emotionally drained from all the demands of his congregation that he has precious little left to give to you. It means being on twenty-four-hour call, yourself as well as your husband. It wreaks havoc with dinner hours and days off and being available to watch your children play baseball or to take them swimming."

Steve took a very deep breath and let it out, and shifted his gaze from the distance to Serena's face. His jaw hardened as he admitted, "Oh yes, Serena, I would like to have a wife, but I don't think such a woman is out there for me."

They walked further into the graveyard, neither speaking, until Steve stopped at a particular stone, a rather new one lying beneath a young poplar tree. He gazed down at it for such a long time that Serena finally took note of whose it was: "Stacia Shepherd," was carved in elaborate script on the stone.

Serena felt Steve's pain. Even though she did not know the whole story of his marriage with Stacia, obviously they had had serious problems that had left this wonderful man wounded and afraid to love again.

"How did she die?" Serena asked quietly.

"Leukemia—complicated I think by a broken heart."

He turned abruptly and strode along the path to the parking lot, where he went to the car and stood by the passenger door waiting for Serena.

She slid into the seat, her heart heavy, not knowing what to say to make the moment pass, to make Steve happy again. Forgotten for the moment was her own discomfort at his being a pastor. Now, he was just a man, like any other, capable of hurt and sorrow. She wanted to take him in her arms.

six

They drove again but only for a short distance, until Steve turned the car off the highway. Serena saw a sign that read, "Elachee Nature Center." The narrow road led to a parking lot where Steve stopped, and they got out.

"This is a natural history museum," he explained as they walked past a variety of flowers toward the large stone building, "and the special place I was going to bring you. I thought you would enjoy the exhibits and botanical gardens. Walking on the trails takes you out of the real world and puts you into nature's."

"You were right—I would enjoy all that, but for now why don't we just walk," Serena suggested, and Steve gave her a nod of approval and diverted her away from the building and onto a path. Red markers marked the way as they began a slow descent from the ridge, the trail meandering through hardwoods and mixed pines, passing lush vegetation of ferns and wild flowers.

"This leads to Walnut Creek," Steve said, and they walked in silence, each lost in their own thoughts.

I should have known he was in a caring profession—a counselor or teacher or minister, Serena thought. *He exudes love and concern for others. That's what first attracted me to him.*

The sound of water reached Serena's ears, and when she saw the creek, she felt better. Flowing water always helped her relax.

They walked beside the creek, then found a bench and sat down. "Tell me about your career," Steve suggested.

"How did you get started? Where did you study? When did you know you had great talent?"

Serena laughed. "Answering all those questions could take awhile."

Steve crossed his arms over his chest and stretched his legs in front of him, crossing them at the ankle. "Fine. I've got all day. I promised Miss Vivian I would not go near my office, and that's exactly what I'm going to do."

Serena murmured her approval of that decision, and tucked one of her legs beneath her, the skirt of her lacy white dress flowing nearly to the ground. With a sigh of contentment, flavored by the sound of the trickling water and the calls of birds, she began, "I was born."

Steve laughed and gave her such an impish grin her heart lurched. She could have laid her head on his shoulder at that moment. She could have touched his face. But she didn't. "I began singing early," she said instead, "and wanted to have lessons, but my parents persuaded me to take piano first, which I did for about three years, starting when I was nine. When I was thirteen, which is still early to begin formal coaching, they found me a vocal teacher at the Kansas City Conservatory of Music. We were living in Missouri at the time."

"Did you enjoy lessons?"

"With all my heart. Robert Vernon was my teacher and he was strict but encouraging. We had a three-week routine: the first week he gave me a new song and we went over it. The second week we worked through it rigorously, polishing it. By the third week, I had to have it memorized."

"Memorized? I'm terrible at that."

"It was fine training for a singer."

Steve turned toward her and laid his arm across the back of the bench, his hand close to her shoulder, but not touching it. "Did you always want to be in opera?" he asked her.

Serena cocked her head to one side, her long hair flowing over his hand. "I originally wanted to be in musical comedy theater—on Broadway. But then I saw my first performance of *Madama Butterfly*, and I knew opera was my home."

"Was it a long road to success?" He felt the strands of her hair on his hand, and was tempted to move his fingers into it. He knew it would be soft. It smelled wonderful.

"Yes, it *was* a long road to success," she answered him, "and a hard one. I didn't just fall into stardom. I had to pay my dues with long years of study, hundreds of recitals, thousands of hours of practice—"

"But you loved it."

"Most of the time, although some days I hated it and felt like I was in prison. Then I would decide to be a waitress or a mechanic—anything that had nothing to do with music."

She sighed deeply and looked over at him. "But music was in my soul, put there by God Himself, I'm sure, and I knew that was my calling," she smiled, "just as you have a calling to the ministry."

Steve nodded, feeling strangely relaxed and exhilarated at the same time. The moment was golden, as they silently enjoyed each other's company, and he was glad he had agreed to take the famous opera diva on a tour of Graylin. However, sitting on a bench with her before a rippling creek, hearing the songs of the birds, becoming lost in the sound of her voice and the color of her glorious green eyes, had not been in the plan. Yet, here he was, and he wanted to be nowhere else.

His heart had not sung this way for such a long time. *But why, Lord, am I so attracted to a woman with whom*

I have nothing in common but a love of fine music, although she does have some kind of spiritual experience?

Steve's practical nature told him just to relax and enjoy the day. It would soon be over, and then Serena would be in the hands of Vivian and the Arts Council and he would see little of her. He would be busy with his church responsibilities and she would be preparing, he hoped, for a concert.

End of association.

Serena's stomach rumbled, and she flushed in embarrassment and sat up with a start. "Oh, I'm so sorry."

Steve laughed and taking her hand, helped her to her feet. "No, I'm the one who should be sorry." He looked at his watch. "Here it is almost two o'clock, and I haven't fed you yet."

He was hardly aware he was touching her. Helping her from the bench seemed the natural thing to do. Her skin was soft, her hand small. A sensation like quickfire raced through him, and now he was suddenly very aware he was touching her.

"You promised me Victor's," she reminded him sweetly, gazing up at him with such a captivating expression he wanted to take her in his arms.

"That I did," he agreed, and they began the ascent to the ridge and the parking lot, where they got in the car and drove to Dean Street.

"You also promised we would walk along this beautiful avenue," she said while staring raptly at the exquisite Victorian homes.

Steve hesitated before saying, "Yes, I remember."

At the time he made the promise it had been a simple enough one. Now, though, he wondered whether or not he should be with Serena that long, for his attraction to her was growing by the minute, and he knew almost nothing about her spiritual life.

Yes, at the time he had first met her, she had asked him if he believed in God, and then told him she did, too, but believing in God was not the same as being a believer in Jesus Christ. Was Serena Lawrence truly a Christian?

How many times had he warned the young people of the church not to date unbelievers. "You are setting yourself up for trouble," he'd said. "The temptation to overlook another person's lack of spirituality can be great if that person is especially nice," he'd said. "It's better to avoid temptation right at the beginning."

He'd believed those words; he believed them still. Living up to them was something else, though. He wanted to take all afternoon lunching with Serena Lawrence, if the truth be told, and he wanted to walk beside her down the street, hear her melodious voice, and smell her perfume.

Preaching to other people had been easy. But now, could he be the Christian example he was supposed to be? He had to know where Serena stood with the Lord.

He pulled into the parking lot of Victor's but didn't get out of the car right away. Instead, he turned to face her and saw the question in her eyes.

"Serena, I have to ask you a question."

"Yes?"

Lord, help me, he prayed. *Give me the words. I don't want to offend her, but I need to be your witness. I don't dare go further in this relationship until I know we share faith in You.*

"Are you a Christian?" he asked simply.

seven

"Yes, I am a believer," Serena answered, "and have been since I was a child. But I have doubts about some things. Is that wrong?"

"No, not wrong, as long as it doesn't lead to unbelief." He paused, then asked, "What things do you doubt?"

She stared out the front window of the car. "I doubt whether God is really in control of our lives."

"Do you mean, Does he make everything happen that happens?"

"Yes."

Steve shook his head. "God has a plan for our lives, just as any parent has for his child, but He does not force that plan upon us. We have free will. We can accept God's leading, or reject it. That's the beauty of our relationship with Him. It can also be the horror."

Serena was silent for a long time and Steve gave her the space she needed to organize her thoughts. Finally, she said, "I haven't spoken about my faith with anyone for years." She turned thoughtful eyes to Steve. "Perhaps I could with you. Sometime."

"If you want."

They got out of the car, and Steve decided a walk together would be good. It might give Serena a chance to express her feelings to him, and he wanted to know more about her. Much more.

They started at the post office and sauntered along the broad, tree-lined street, gazing at the two- and three-storied white Victorian and Neo-classical homes. Set back far from the sidewalk, supported by tall, white pillars, and surrounded by expansive green lawns, they spoke of the end of the 19th century and the beginning of the 20th, when Graylin had its share of wealthy people and this was the most prestigious street on which to live.

"Graylin was created in 1821," Steve told her, "and used to be a gathering place for traders and Indians."

"Indians?"

"Yes. North Georgia was home to the Cherokee until 1838 and there are names all around us of rivers and towns that remind us of those days: Chattahoochee, Chestatee, Amicalola Falls, Dahlonega, Hiawassee."

The walking tour took more than twenty minutes, and Steve told Serena more about his hometown and answered questions she brought up, but Serena said nothing of her beliefs, and Steve did not broach the subject. When she was ready, he knew from years of counseling, she would tell him. Till then, he would wait.

Victor's was at the end of their walk, and the quaint beige-colored house with green awnings was not crowded when they entered.

"Do you eat here often?" Serena asked Steve as they were led to their table by a handsome, young waiter wearing a burgundy shirt and black slacks. The waiter smiled at them and was about to pull out Serena's chair for her, but Steve stepped in and did it first.

"Not often, I'd have to say," Steve answered, "though it is a favorite. Graylin has a wide variety of restaurants serving all kinds of food in all price ranges, and I've tried most of them."

Serena raised her eyebrows. "Are you a member of the Chamber of Commerce as well as the Arts Council?"

"No, ma'am. My plate's full enough without that responsibility. Excuse the pun. I'm just a man who can't cook."

He grinned, showing his dimples, and Serena's heart

skipped a beat. *No pastor should be that adorable,* she thought, and then laughed, feeling comfortable with him again, hoping he would not pry into a subject that was a tender one for her. She had bad memories that had to do with the church, and she tried not to recall them, ever, even though they dealt with her mother.

She studied the menu for some time, aware that Steve was watching her, which made her breathing quicken and her mind refuse to focus on what she wanted to eat. Finally, she chose a vegetable quiche, and Steve ordered a crab salad, and they carried on a conversation of small talk.

Part of Steve's mind was on what they were talking about—the weather, aspects of life in Graylin, the musical culture of the town—but in between dialogue he thought again of the vague answer he had received from Serena about being a believer. It troubled him.

A majority of Americans claimed to be believers, but most had no idea what a true commitment to Christ meant. He hoped Serena was not one of those. He wanted her to be sure of her salvation. He wanted. . .he stopped his mental gymnastics, knowing where they were taking him.

Even if she were the Lord's most devoted follower, prayed and read her Bible every day, went to church twice on Sunday, and handed out gospel tracts at Rockefeller Center—it would not matter to the future of their relationship. There could be no relationship. Their worlds were eons apart. To enjoy each other's company more than they already had was pointless, and could be dangerous. In a few days or weeks she would be gone, never to return, and he would be here, and still lonely for a woman of his own. For her.

"So," he started up the conversation that had lagged, "where are you off to next?" He wanted to know, wanted to remind himself how unattainable she was. Wanted to protect his heart.

He sensed her relief at discussing something less sensitive than her faith, or lack thereof.

"I'm to record an album in New York soon," she said, hoping that would be true, and leaving out the fact that she had postponed it just that morning. Her voice was too strained. She dared not risk it now on a brutal eight hours or longer of recording.

"Then, in the fall, there's a performance of *Madama Butterfly* in London." That commitment she *had* to fulfill.

"That's your signature role," Steve said with enthusiasm. "Have you seen it?"

"Yes, and you in it, Serena. On television. You're wonderful," he said softly, his eyes capturing hers. "I've heard other Butterflies—but you're the best. The very best."

Serena held her breath, having received thousands of compliments during her career, but knowing none was more sincere than the one Steve had just given her. "It's kind of you to say so," she responded, hoping the tremor in her voice was not giving away her emotions.

"We will certainly understand if you decide you don't have time to give a concert here."

"But I want to," she decided eagerly, and rashly. "You have shown me how many groups there are in your wonderful city who are dedicated to the fine arts, and that you need a performing arts center. I would like to help you raise the money."

A smile burst onto Steve's face. "That's great news, Serena. You will be doing a tremendous thing for this community."

"I'll tell Miss Vivian when we get back, and we'll select a date. Perhaps two months from now would be good," she suggested. "That would allow time for advertising and promotion."

And give my voice a chance to recuperate from

whatever is plaguing it, she thought. *Two months. Surely that should be enough time. I'll call my doctor tomorrow and tell him the news. He'll be pleased to hear it, and I'll follow his advice to the letter.*

They finished eating, and Steve pulled back her chair as they prepared to leave.

"Would you like to announce the concert tomorrow night when the Chorale sings?" Serena asked.

Steve paid the bill. "Great idea, but Miss Vivian would be the one to do it. I probably won't be there."

Serena stopped halfway through the door and turned to him in surprise. They were so close she could see the tiny flecks of gold in his eyes and hear his breath. "Not be there? But I thought you were going to escort me?"

"I think I've monopolized your company long enough," he said. "There are many others who will happily take my place."

He placed his hand on the small of her back and nudged her through the door and toward the parking lot. Serena felt the weight of his touch and her blood raced through her body. She knew for a certainty that she wanted Steve to accompany her to the Chorale concert. She wanted to be with Steve, not a stranger from the Arts Council.

Before getting into the car, she turned and faced him and boldly said, "Please go with me, Steve."

Her voice was husky, her breathing quickened. She knew she was taking a step beyond that of a mere acquaintance. She wondered how Steve would react to her making clear that she liked him more than as a tour guide for the Arts Council.

Steve did not answer right away, as Serena waited to see if he felt the same way about her. He had told her there was no one special in his life, hadn't he? What would be wrong with him taking her to hear the Chorale?

"Serena," he said gently, "I'm not going to pretend I

don't want to be with you, for I do." He leaned toward her and she smelled the masculine scent of his cologne. "But I always stay home on Saturday nights, to prepare for Sunday, go over my sermon, pray for the congregation. I hope you understand."

Her eyes flashed. "I don't. You asked me in the first place, Steve."

"Yes."

"Now you are rescinding your offer? Why?"

He suddenly took both her shoulders in his hands and said forcefully, "You know why."

And she did.

They were attracted to each other, strongly attracted, and if he were any other man he would be kissing her now. But he was not like other men. He was different. He had a calling from God to preach the gospel, a calling to minister to the flock of his church, and he and Serena both knew there was no place in his life for a celebrity who traveled the world.

He was ending their relationship before it even began, turning away from a potential heartbreak before it was allowed to happen. He was strong, and right, but oh, how Serena resented that strength. She pulled back from him and got in the car, her mouth set firmly. She would not throw herself at this minister, as if he were the only man available.

When Steve closed his door, he turned to her and said, "You do understand what I'm doing, don't you, Serena?"

"Of course," she replied without looking at him. "I shall be perfectly happy to go with Miss Vivian."

Though Steve tried to talk with her on the way to Vivian's, Serena's answers were stiff and unnatural.

I've hurt her, he berated himself, *but it's better now than later. It's foolish to tease ourselves that we can ever be anything more than acquaintances.*

eight

Serena went to the Chorale with Miss Vivian, enjoyed it tremendously, and was impressed with the artistic quality of the group. She was introduced to various members of the Board of Directors of the Graylin Arts Council and agreed to meet them the next week to determine the details of the concert she would give. They were, of course, ecstatic with her decision.

Steve was not there, and Serena was disappointed, but told herself it was for the best. What would be the point in following her heart and allowing her feelings for him to grow? Eventually she would have to say goodbye, and that would hurt too much.

As she and Miss Vivian circulated through the large foyer of the church, talking to people who came up to them, two young women hurried past. One was short, with kinky brown hair, a pug nose, and heavy shoes that clunked on the polished wooden floor, but pretty enough in a plain dress of black chiffon; while the other, wearing a form-fitting dress of white silk-crepe, caught Serena's attention because of her long black hair that hung halfway down her back. They were giggling about something but stopped when Miss Vivian called out, "Did you enjoy the Chorale, Mary?"

The dark-haired girl turned and smiled with plump, red lips sliding over gleaming white teeth. Her eyebrows were as dark as her hair, her skin white and smooth.

"Yes, Ma'am," she responded in a sweet, high-pitched

voice, her eyes sparkling. "It was wonderful." She gave a little wave. "See you tomorrow in church." She and the other girl moved on through the lobby and out the front doors.

"That Mary Upton," Miss Vivian said, almost to herself, as she took Serena's arm and led her in the same direction, "has certainly grown up in the last two years. I can't imagine that scamp teaching at stuffy old Everitt Academy, but I hear she's doing an admirable job."

Mary Upton. The name struck a note in Serena's memory, and she wished she had paid more attention to the young woman Walter Thomas, the deacon, thought would make a good wife for Steve Shepherd. How did Steve feel about her? she wondered.

On Sunday, Miss Vivian went to church—Steve's church—and asked Serena if she would like to go, too.

"Thank you, but no," Serena declined, giving no reason, and Miss Vivian did not press for one.

The morning was long for Serena, who spent it reading in the gazebo while trying to keep her mind from imagining what was happening at Steve's church. What were his people like? Was Steve a good preacher? Was he popular with the congregation?

Oh, yes, she decided, he would have to be loved by them. Wasn't he strong and decent? Intelligent and compassionate? Didn't he have a sense of humor and a gift for understanding the troubled spirit?

She daydreamed the morning away, listening to the constant chatter of birds in the trees, watching butterflies dance from flower to flower, enjoying the third day of the first vacation she had had in years.

She puttered around Miss Vivian's house in comfortable peach-colored slacks and matching shirt, content to be by herself, and began writing a letter to her father to explain where she would be for awhile. She even vocalized for ten minutes and felt no strain in doing so.

When Miss Vivian returned, she found lunch waiting— a simple pasta salad with fresh-cooked broccoli, garlic toast, and cut fruit. "I raided your refrigerator," Serena explained. She felt a tinge of guilt for not asking permission first, but Miss Vivian was pleased she had felt enough at home to do so.

They ate on the sun porch at a white wicker table. Serena was amused to see that although Miss Vivian was dressed in a lovely outfit, and even had earrings on and a bracelet, she was barefoot.

"When spring is close to summer, and the weather gets warm, it's time to go barefoot," Miss Vivian declared after noticing Serena's glances toward her feet. "Growing up, we girls always had to wait until Mother said it was all right to do so. One just did not go barefoot at any old time of the year. We would watch her, day after day, in eager anticipation of The Time."

"The Time?"

"When she would sit in her chair by the front window, slip one foot out of its shoe, wiggle her toes as though to test the air for warmth, and then say, 'It's time.' We would scream with glee, kick our shoes off, and hope they wouldn't land in the nearest plant, or up on a table to knock something over. Mother would pretend to be disgusted with us over our hollerin'."

Miss Vivian looked down at Serena's expensive leather sandals. "Would you like to go barefoot?" she asked.

Serena chuckled. "I can't remember the last time I did," but she quickly wiggled out of the shoes, held her feet up off the ground, wiggled her toes and turned her ankles, and finally declared. "It's time." Then she laughed out loud, and so did Miss Vivian, and they went on with their delightful lunch.

"Stephen preached a fine sermon this morning, on setting priorities," Miss Vivian said casually, sipping on her glass of sweetened iced tea. "He used the text from Mark 8, 'For what will it profit a man if he gains the whole world, and loses his own soul?' I've never heard him better. Of course, Stephen is one of the most articulate preachers in town. He has a reputation for understanding the human heart and bringing God's Word to focus on our everyday lives. He can make us laugh, or cry. Mostly, though, he encourages us to believe in ourselves, and in the fact that God loves us and wants only the best for us."

"You sound well-pleased to have him."

"I am. We are. We hope Stephen stays with us forever. Why, we've grown from 200 members to over 2,000 since he's been our pastor."

"Really?"

Miss Vivian nodded. "Our youth department has quadrupled. Young people love Stephen. He's straight forward and honest with them, but understanding of their needs and drives."

Serena remembered the many questions about life and God that she had had while growing up in the church. Unfortunately, her pastor had been distant and out of touch, so she had relied more on the advice of her mother and father, particularly her mother. *Mom always could explain things to me,* she thought with a pang of sadness.

Losing her mother to cancer when she was only fourteen had been a terrible blow to Serena, a blow she'd never completely gotten over. *Why, God? Why did I have to lose my mother just when I needed her the most?*

"Of course, the senior citizens adore him, too," Miss Vivian was saying. "Now, if we could just find him the perfect wife. . . ."

She let the thought hang on the air, and Serena remembered Steve telling her that Miss Vivian, as well as Walter Thomas, was searching for a wife for him.

What would the perfect woman be for Steve? Serena pondered, *and do Vivian and Walter want her to be perfect for Steve, or for the church?*

"Does Steve want a wife?" she was surprised to hear herself ask.

Miss Vivian quickly responded, "Yes, and no. He *needs* a wife, that's the truth, to help him in the church, and to be a companion, but he's gotten stubborn lately about finding one. 'I don't have time,' he says. 'I don't know anyone well enough.' Bosh! He just isn't trying."

Miss Vivian stood up and stacked the dishes, and Serena helped her take them into the kitchen. Miss Vivian washed them by hand, and Serena dried them.

"He was married once, you know," Miss Vivian explained. "A nice enough girl, Stacia, but not all that interested in the church. She wanted the prestige of being the pastor's wife, but not the responsibility."

"Were they happy together?" Serena asked.

Miss Vivian paused while putting the iced tea glasses up on the shelf, and said slowly, "I . . . think so. They never quarreled in front of anyone, but there wasn't a . . . spark there, either. I'm sure they liked each other, but I doubt there was much passion."

Passion, Serena thought. *Passion with Steve. What would that be like?*

She had been drawn to him the moment they'd been introduced. She'd felt a tingle when he'd touched her. Her heart quickened now whenever he looked at her intently. *How easily he has drawn me to himself*, she thought, *while we are still relative strangers. What would*

*it be like if we were married? If there were no restraints.
If we were free to love, to hold each other, to kiss—*

"He needs children, too," Miss Vivian was saying. "He's
so good with the ones at church, always taking time for
them, tossing them into the air, admiring a little girl's
pretty dress, roughhousing with the boys." She shook her
head sadly. "There's a lot of love locked up in that man
that needs to come out." She looked at Serena. "He needs
to fall desperately in love, with a woman as committed to
the Lord as he is. That's the key. We need to find someone
spiritually mature."

"Is there no one he's interested in?" Serena asked, hoping her question sounded a casual one.

Miss Vivian thought for a moment or two, then said, "I
don't believe there's anyone at the moment, but there are
several fine young women in the church who would suit
him well." She winked at Serena. "How to get him to
pick one of them is the next step."

Serena smiled, but in her heart she wondered just what
kind of woman Steve would pick for a wife; she did not
doubt that a man as virile and compassionate as he would
eventually find someone who suited him. *Lucky girl*, she
thought.

They were finished with the dishes, and Serena was
finished with her silly daydreaming, she decided. She had
been thinking of Steve in strictly physical ways, ways
she as an artist, as a passionate woman, could satisfy him.
What she could not give him, though, was the spiritual
companion he needed, not when she felt the way she did
about the church.

Oh, for goodness sake, she railed silently, *what am I
thinking of? I barely know the man.*

She followed Miss Vivian into the living room, where
they watched an old rerun of *I Love Lucy*. Then Miss Vivian

went off to take her afternoon nap, and Serena finished her letter to her father and then called her doctor at his home in Connecticut.

He was delighted with her determination to rest for a month or two, but ended their conversation by saying, "Remember, Serena, there are no guarantees. Rest may or may not solve your problem. Time will tell."

Dismayed at so uncertain a verdict for her future, Serena went for a long walk and pondered what she might do with the rest of her life if she could not sing. The possibility was too frightening to think about long.

The Board of Directors of the Graylin Arts Council met the following Tuesday morning, for a special session to discuss the Serena Lawrence concert, and were ecstatic to learn that Serena wanted to *donate* her time and talent for the endeavor, so that one hundred percent of the revenue could go toward building the performing arts center.

"We thank you on behalf of all artists and audiences who will benefit from your most generous gift," Miss Vivian said at the close of the meeting, "and I know each member of the Council will give you full support in promoting the concert."

They decided to hold the concert June 24th at the Georgia Mountains Center which could seat 2600 people, and where the acoustics would more than adequately compliment Miss Lawrence's voice. Ticket prices would range from four to twenty dollars, Serena having insisted on the lower-prices to accommodate those lovers of opera who found it difficult to pay the exorbitant prices often asked for celebrity concerts. The Council agreed, for they were sure the concert would be a sellout, thus putting them well on their way to funding the center. Any more money that was needed, they hoped would be donated by civic-minded local companies.

Steve was there but said nothing during the brief meeting, although he wanted to when he was assigned the task of coordinating television, radio, and newspaper interviews for Miss Lawrence. He knew this meant they would be spending a lot of time together, but he also knew he could hardly say no to the Council. He smiled grimly to himself, imagining the reaction if he told the Council that Serena Lawrence was a temptation he should avoid.

He watched the other Council members hover around her, thanking her, wanting to get to know her, inviting her to their homes for dinner or lunch or tea once they learned she would be vacationing there until the concert. Some were even asking for her autograph.

She was wearing an aqua jumpsuit with long sleeves and a wide belt that accented her small waist and suited the coloring of her skin and hair. Today her shining auburn hair was pulled back from her face in a thick French twist—so elegant, as she herself was elegant.

Steve moved around the fringe of the crowd that surrounded her, not commenting, but catching Serena's eye from time to time. Whenever she gave him a shy smile, his heart quickened. He watched her give her attention completely to each person who spoke to her, and he admired her graciousness and genuine caring.

"She *is* lovely, isn't she?" Miss Vivian commented softly beside him, and he looked down at her. She wore a paisley dress with short, puffy sleeves that gave her a youthful look. He had seen it many times, for Miss Vivian was not a wealthy woman, but she did buy good clothing and had fashion sense and always looked as though she were a woman of means and style. In her eyes he saw the glow of satisfaction that shows when one has accomplished something worthwhile, and getting Serena Lawrence to give a benefit performance in Graylin had to rank as the number one coups of the year.

"Yes, she is lovely," he agreed.

"She will be a joy to work with, as you have already discovered."

"That she will."

"I asked her to come to church with me last Sunday, but she declined."

"She was probably tired."

The eyes of his dear friend looked into his. "Is she not a Christian, Stephen?"

He exhaled deep and slowly. "She says she is, but has been out of fellowship for awhile. I sense there's an unresolved problem there rather than disinterest."

"Good. Then we'll work on her."

"We?" A pang of anxiety told him Miss Vivian was planning something he was not sure he should be a part of.

"Yes," she said, we—thee and me." There was a tiny smile on her mouth.

nine

"Now, Miss Vivian. . . ," Steve warned.

"Sweet Serena is a lost sheep who needs to return to the fold," his friend replied.

"Probably."

"And lost sheep, though lovable, need a good shepherd."

"Yes."

She turned to him, her huge doe-brown eyes dancing. "Stephen dear, you are the finest shepherd I know."

Steve began to panic. "Miss Vivian, you're not playing matchmaker, are you?"

A look of amazement replaced the whimsical one. "Playing?" she questioned, raising her finely-shaped eyebrows toward the soft white hair on her head. "Absolutely not. Playing is what one does in a game where the outcome is not all that important to time and eternity. When I matchmake, Pastor Shepherd, it is serious business, and since I'm so very fond of you, I'm going to give this my most serious attention."

"Miss Vivian—"

"I like Serena very much, Stephen, and between the two of us we need to be sure she is living God's plan for her life."

"I don't think—"

"Oh, don't worry," she interrupted him gently, not taking her eyes from Serena whom she'd been watching, "we're not going to coerce her."

"Good."

"After all, Stephen, you and I are both Southern, blessed

to have been born and raised here, just like our fathers and grandfathers before us. We'll just move slowly, methodically, and help Serena Lawrence to recognize the common sense in her staying here, too."

"Miss Vivian, I won't. . . ," Steve started to say, but she moved away to Serena, and he couldn't shout after her what he'd been going to say—I won't be a party to your shenanigans—not that it would have mattered to Miss Vivian even if he had said it. With or without his approval, he knew she was going on with her plan.

"Heaven help me," he groaned, and went to give his thanks to Serena, as every other Council member had done.

"Why don't you go to Stephen's office and discuss publicity," Miss Vivian suggested when all the other Council members had left and just the three of them were walking out to their cars.

Serena looked at Steve and knew what was going through his mind. He was obligated to help the Arts Council, but he would have preferred doing it in a way that kept him away from personal contact with her. While she admired his ability to make a decision and stick by it, she was sad they could not get to know each other better. He was a fine man, this Pastor Shepherd, strong, respected, committed to serving others, and handsome as a film star, not to mention a charming Southern gentleman whose deep voice and barely perceptible accent were music to her ears.

It would be so easy to fall in love with him, she thought. *So easy*.

She thought back on when she was an emotional teenager and fell in love every other day. How uncomplicated her love life had been then: she met a boy she liked and gave him her heart. Simple. Maybe the relationship would last two months, or two weeks, or, more likely, two hours, but she was free to pursue it with all her heart, come what may.

Now, though, she was older, mature, settled into a demanding career that took most of her emotional energy to survive in it, and left little time or inclination for a brief fling. Life was too serious now to complicate it with a man who had a calling to serve a God she resented more than she worshipped.

"That's fine with me," Steve said in answer to Miss Vivian's suggestion that they go to his office.

Serena blinked. "It is?"

"Sure."

His genial expression assured her that he meant it, and when their eyes met, their hearts seemed to meet also. She softly said, "All right."

"I'd love to join you two," Miss Vivian said, "but I have Bible study in a half hour." She turned to Serena. "Even though it's held in our church, it's a community group, nondenominational. Women from many different churches attend. Perhaps you'd like to come next week as my guest."

"I think I'd like that," Serena answered sincerely. She had always loved reading the Bible and had done so consistently when she'd been younger. For too long now she'd allowed daily pressures to rob her of that special time with God, and she was sorry for that. *Perhaps at this study I'll find the answers to some of my questions about Him*, she thought.

"Why don't I come with you now, Miss Vivian," she suggested suddenly. "Then I could meet with Steve later." She turned to him. "If that would work into your schedule?"

He was obviously surprised at her quick decision, but

pleased with it, too, she could tell from his expression, and when he said, "No problem. I'll wait for you in my office," his eyes twinkled. Serena knew she had done a good thing.

There were 120 women who met for the Bible study at Evangelical Community Church, Steve's church, and Miss Vivian introduced Serena to every one of them, Serena was sure. Many of the women knew who she was; others did not. Altogether, they were simply a group of women of all ages from different churches and differing doctrinal beliefs who had a longing to hear and understand God's Word.

Miss Vivian and Serena shared a New King James translation of the Bible, and Serena was amazed to see how marked it was. With yellow highlighter and green felt-tipped pen, Miss Vivian had drawn through or underlined what, to her, were significant verses, and in the margins she had carefully made notes that clarified the text.

Listening to the familiar words she had once known so well, sharing an eagerness with the other women there to learn God's truth, Serena felt as though she had come home. Her heart began to fill with the unique joy that comes from no other source than God's Holy Spirit. She relaxed her mind, forgetting the anxiety of the past several months over the condition of her voice, and let her spirit flow heavenward.

The passage they studied was from Psalm 40, verses 11-13, and it was a lesson about change and how to handle it when it is thrust upon you.

> "Do not withhold Your tender mercies from
>   me, O Lord;
> Let Your lovingkindness and Your
> truth continually preserve me.

For innumerable evils have surrounded
  me;. . .
Therefore my heart fails me.
Be pleased, O Lord, to deliver me;
O Lord, make haste to help me!"

Serena was stunned with the words, for they expressed
exactly the feelings she had had recently, when this un-
known something that was attacking her throat had first
begun to take away her peace. She knew she should have
turned more earnestly to prayer, and to reading God's
Word. While doctors have certain expertise, they cannot
heal the soul and bring the kind of peace that only comes
from a relationship with the Great Physician, Jesus Christ.

Although she had little experience in seeing miracle
cures from God, she knew they existed, and she believed
that such a thing could happen, even in today's world.
Even to her. God's power was no less mighty than it had
been when Christ had walked this earth, and the sick, the
lame, the blind, and numerous others with all manner of
sickness and disease had come to Him for healing—and
He had healed them.

Serena's eyes filled with tears when the leader of the
group asked if there were any prayer requests. She did
not voice hers then, for she still wanted no one to know of
her condition, but when there was a call for unspoken
requests, she tentatively raised her hand as the tears slid
down her cheeks.

Oh Lord, she prayed silently, *You know how concerned
I am—and afraid. I don't know what's the matter with me,
but You do. I ask You for wisdom to deal with this problem and, more specifically, I am boldly asking that You
heal me, dear Lord.*

Her hands were trembling, and she didn't realize she

was sobbing until Miss Vivian reached out and covered her hands with her own. She said nothing to Serena, but Serena felt the concern and caring through her touch, and her heart melted.

Afterward, as they were walking upstairs to Steve's office, Serena waited for Miss Vivian to ask her what had brought on her tears and need for prayer, but the questions never came. Serena knew, though, that if she ever wanted to talk about it, Miss Vivian would be there, to listen and to care.

"How was Bible study?" Steve asked her after they arrived at his office.

"It was wonderful," she answered, and turned away so he couldn't see the mistiness of her eyes.

"Children," Miss Vivian said, "I have some errands to run. Stephen, you *will* bring Serena home, won't you?" and for a woman her age, she was out the door in remarkable time, before either of them could mount an argument.

Serena looked around Steve's office and saw a massive room with forest green carpeting and two solid walls of books, in front of which was a conversation area made up of a three-seater couch, two chairs, and a coffee table. On the other side of the room, in front of an octagonal window that looked out on a small but flourishing flower garden, was a round conference table with six chairs.

She had seen many an office, and knew that it usually accurately represented the personality of its occupant. That proved to be the case here, too, for this office *was* Steve: filled with books (his intelligence indicated he had probably read every one), large (to fit his own size), neat (the papers on his three-section desk were obviously stacked in some kind of order), and accented here and there with memorabilia, which showed the human, emotional side of the man whose awesome responsibility was to be shepherd to over two thousand people. The conference table, with its six chairs, spoke of serious business conducted not by the iron will of the pastor, but by shared thoughts and solutions of the members.

Still, it was a friendly room, the intimidating size of it diffused by comfortable furniture in a green and rust paisley print, healthy green plants, and a number of pictures on the wall of various people with Steve. It was not exactly a room where one would put one's dusty cowboy boots on the coffee table, nor was it so elegant to have a decorator's stamp on it. It was . . .Steve—warm, inviting, friendly, but businesslike and practical, too.

"So you enjoyed the Bible study?" he asked.

"Yes, I did. It was. . .stimulating and thought-provoking." She hoped he could not tell she had been crying, and hastily brushed a finger beneath both eyes, in case some of her mascara had washed down.

"What did you study?" he asked, and Serena told him while he listened with interest.

A small voice in her head told her to share her concerns with Steve, ask his advice for getting through the next few months while the waiting would be agony. Each moment she contemplated doing so made her feel more strongly that she should confide in him—but then the telephone rang.

Steve excused himself, walked over to his desk, and picked up the receiver. "Oh, hello, Mary. . . . I'm sorry, I can't tonight. . . . Yes, I suppose I could see you in a few minutes. . . . Good-bye."

During the conversation, Serena had picked up a bulletin from the previous Sunday's services and in a futile attempt not to listen to what Steve was saying to Mary Upton, she read through the weekly schedule. There was a men's fellowship, six women's circles, a senior high group, junior high, college, singles, young marrieds, senior citizens, support groups for those who were divorced, or had problems with alcohol or drugs, or their families.

She was amazed. The church in which she had grown up had been large and active, but it had not had all the programs this one did. "There is something going on here every day and night of the week," she exclaimed to Steve when he returned from his phone call.

"Our people are active in their faith," he replied.

"Do you supervise all these activities?" she asked, incredulous.

"Supervise, yes. Plan and coordinate, no."

"That still means endless hours. How do you have the time?"

"It's what I'm called to, and what I love to do. God gives me the energy."

"But you're alone. Most ministers have a wife to share the load. You're doing it by yourself."

The words were out of her mouth before Serena thought. Ever since her talk with Miss Vivian, she had wondered how Steve managed without a woman at his side. She realized from the way Steve suddenly frowned that her question was a painful one, and she wished she could call it back, but it was too late to do so.

ten

"You're right in saying a pastor's wife carries a large share of responsibility," he said, his eyes conveying a sadness that touched Serena's heart. "Unfortunately, I've never had such a soul mate."

Serena frowned. "You were married."

"Yes, but Stacia. . . ." He looked out the window, to the garden where a sprinkler system had come on and was bathing the lavender petunias and pink impatiens with a fine mist of water. "Stacia never enjoyed the role thrust upon her by the church, and me. Oh, she thought she would. She assured me of that before we married. She had been active in church affairs all her life, but having the entire congregation look to her for leadership . . . well, it was more than she could handle. She was young, and then she became ill. . .and. . . ."

Serena went to him and laid her hand on his arm, amazed at his confession and filled with sympathy for him. How very long he had been carrying the load himself.

Oh, dear Lord, she sincerely prayed, *isn't there someone You can send to Steve, someone who wants to do Your work as much as he does?*

Steve looked down at her with appreciation and a slight smile, and laid his hand on hers. Serena wanted to put her arms around him, for in this moment, he was not Pastor Shepherd, God's anointed, His called, leader of flock, fount of wisdom. He was, instead, just a man trying, by himself, to do the job of two, and doing brilliantly well at it if the size and activity of the church was any indication.

69

But how long could he continue to do so?

No wonder Miss Vivian and Walter wanted to find him a wife. He needed help. He needed someone unique to share his calling—and give him love. Could that someone be Mary Upton?

Meanwhile, Steve was fighting temptation for all he was worth. He felt Serena's hand on his arm and it seemed to set him on fire. He wanted desperately to pull her into his arms, to feel her warmth. She seemed so understanding of him, so intuitive as to what he needed. Was that because she was an artist of great ability, and therefore, great sensitivity?

He couldn't explain why he'd told her about Stacia. He knew his words had been too personal an admission for someone he barely knew. Since Serena Lawrence had come into his life, things were happening that he could not explain. Feelings were being heightened.

He cleared his throat and said, "Why don't we talk about your publicity." He motioned Serena toward the conference table and grabbed a notebook and pen from his desk.

"I imagine you have a publicist," he confirmed, noting the vibrancy of her jade-colored eyes.

"Yes, in New York. She has my biography, black and white or color photos, audio and video clips for radio and television."

"That will make my job a whole lot easier." Her lips looked so soft, so pretty, tinged with a light peach color.

"Well, it's a start. We'll need to localize the material."

"Change it some for each interview."

"Scheduling will take time."

"Of course I'll take you to the stations or papers here and in the towns around us."

"I'll appreciate that."

"It will be my pleasure."

He stared at her a long time, then reached out and took her hand. It was warm, matching the way she was looking back at him—expectant, attuned, her whole attention on him.

"So," he said carefully, "why were you crying at the Bible study?"

Serena was surprised at his question and lowered her eyes to study their locked hands. Inside her, a wall went up. It could have been a physical one, Steve felt it so profoundly. Whatever had brought tears to her eyes was more than momentary emotion at reading a meaningful passage of Scripture. It was something serious, and Steve regretted having pushed his way into it instead of waiting for her to come to him about it.

"I withdraw the question," he said gently.

Serena's eyes flashed in a burst of temper. "Good, because it's none of your business, or anyone else's."

Thinking about her publicity and the interviews ahead had made her remember the natural tenacity of reporters to get a unique story. What if one of them should cleverly get her to reveal the real reason she was in Graylin—not to do a concert, but to rest her voice?

Then she could hear a reporter's question: "Are you beyond your prime, Miss Lawrence?" Or read the headline: "Opera Diva's Voice No Longer Able to Take the Strain of an International Career."

It would be over, then, being on top, being one of the most sought-after sopranos in the world, for once there was even a suspicion her voice was not in perfect form, she would be judged differently. Now, she was invincible, flawless performances her hallmark, but then, every critic would hear a flaw even where there wasn't one, and her career would be destroyed.

She saw the surprise and hurt in Steve's eyes at her

sharp and rude remark. He, like Miss Vivian, was only showing concern. She knew he wasn't prying.

She raised Steve's hand to her cheek and pressed against it. "I'm so sorry," she apologized. "Now you know I have a temper."

His eyes were alert, but not condemning. "I know you have a burden that's hard to carry. Just know that I'm here for you if you need me."

Indecision raced through Serena. Oh, how she wanted to share her fears with him. What a relief to have some-one to talk with about it.

But she couldn't. It was safer not to. She would rest her voice, talk less, vocalize far less, give this one concert, and she'd be back to normal again. Yes, she would.

Steve stood up. "I know just what you need." A big smile, showing his dimples, broke the somber mood Serena had fallen into.

"And what might that be?" she asked.

"Two slices of fresh strawberry pie from Shoney's," he declared.

Serena stood up, too, and exclaimed, "*Two* slices?"

"Maybe I'll buy you the whole pie so you can take it home."

She shook her head back and forth. "If I gain ten pounds from eating this marvelous creation, will the Arts Coun-cil want a fat soprano to sing for them?"

Steve burst out laughing. "Lady, they'll take you any way they can get you—fat or otherwise. Why, even if you were pleasingly plump, there'd just be more of you to—"

He suddenly stopped as they both mentally finished the sentence, and then he added, in a whisper she barely heard: "to love." He bent down and kissed her, gently, lingering, savoring their first intimacy.

The door to his office opened, but neither Steve nor Serena noticed who was there, for his arms had slid around Serena and he was kissing her again, with more intensity, and she was kissing him back and clinging to his shoulders as her knees weakened.

A tiny gasp, from a woman, made Serena open her eyes, only to see the back of someone hurrying away, closing the door behind her. In that glimpse, Serena recognized the long dark hair of Mary Upton, and could only imagine what she must be thinking, having found her pastor kissing a stranger in his office.

But then she thought no more of her, for Steve was cupping her face in his hands and saying, "You are the most incredible woman I have ever known."

But not the most honest, Serena added to herself, knowing she should not allow him to care for her, or let herself grow fond of him.

She was not good at saying good-byes, and in just a few short weeks she would be saying just that to Steve Shepherd. She didn't want to break his heart—or her own.

They walked out of his office, and Steve hoped their time together would bring Serena confidence in him so she could share the terrible hurt that was festering inside her.

Serena was glad to be going, too, but also glad that Steve did not know about her voice, the secret she must keep, a secret that could jeopardize the very reason she was in Graylin.

eleven

The days drifted by, and Serena relaxed into a routine. She rose at seven and made her own breakfast, then took a book or the latest issue of *Opera Magazine* out to the gazebo where she read for an hour. During the day she did things she rarely had time for when she was touring: shopping in the mall, buying groceries, going to a movie, or just walking around the block.

Though Miss Vivian had offered her the use of her car, Serena rented one of her own, a two-seater luxury sports model, red, which she drove with great relish.

Having no set schedule, able to do whatever she wanted, whenever she wanted, brought her immense enjoyment. She realized that most of the time her life was rigidly structured and almost entirely focused around the world of music, to the point where she rarely met an average person or knew what that person did with his or her life. Little things became a delight, like buying an ice cream cone and sitting on a bench in a park to watch mothers and small children at play; or having the time to browse through a bookstore, reading the blurbs on the backs of whatever books interested her; or not having to study music and memorize foreign words and eat late at night.

"I'm not used to being free," she told Miss Vivian. "It's exciting."

"Most people envy your fame and success," her hostess replied, "without realizing the harsh discipline required to get to that pinnacle."

"Oh, don't misunderstand—I chose my career and

74

willingly gave up everything else for it. I've never wanted to do anything else but sing."

Miss Vivian smiled. "You are also a woman who needs to have a good time, do things just for yourself. When was the last time you were silly?"

Serena laughed heartily. "I'm never silly, only serious."

A strange look came into Miss Vivian's eyes. "I'm going to have to talk to Stephen about that."

Serena wondered what on earth she meant by that.

She started to write. A publisher had offered her a six-figure contract for her life's story, but she had said no. She was far too busy performing to have time to put down on paper her climb from an ordinary, skinny girl of thirteen, to one of the leading sopranos of the world, and she would not use a ghost writer. So, the project had been shelved.

Until now. Until she was forced not to sing for awhile, and even to curtail her speaking.

Dr. Jeffries had suggested she vocalize only every other day, and for just twenty minutes at a time, and also to speak as little as possible, being careful not to whisper, which could be worse on her vocal cords than talking out loud. Serena wanted to follow his advice, but knew she could never give a concert with so little practice. She needed to keep her voice supple, fine-tuned, so she vocalized twice a day for twenty minutes, being careful to warm up first with light exercises. *Surely that's not too much strain*, she told herself, and indeed the quality of her voice seemed to bear out her supposition.

To justify being alone for long periods so she wouldn't have to use her voice by speaking to anyone, she decided to begin the manuscript of her life.

"What a wonderful project," Miss Vivian said. She promised not to disturb Serena when she was writing, but was disappointed her star guest was not more available for parties and luncheons and introductions. She knew, however, the diva needed private time, a change of pace from the rigorous scheduling that could have her performing on four continents in just one month, and she determined to give it to her.

There were, though, quiet talks between the two of them, usually in the late afternoon, and they always watched the evening news together. Miss Vivian became very fond of this young woman who was so appreciative of her hospitality. Serena even continued to cook for them both, though she was not very experienced at it.

Miss Vivian rarely heard Serena singing, and she was surprised that Serena did not do so at a certain time each day, having thought that singers of her magnitude were strictly disciplined in such matters. She concluded Serena was breaking with all normal routine and was practicing whenever she was gone, which was a disappointment, for Miss Vivian would have loved to listen.

The first Sunday she was there, Serena had declined Miss Vivian's invitation to accompany her to church, but on the second Sunday she agreed, and Vivian was glad. She knew there was a spark of something between Serena and Stephen, and even though she would love to have lived up to Stephen's fear that she was matchmaking, she doubted a long-term commitment was possible between them. So, she decided the next best thing was a time of old-fashioned affection, the kind she had always enjoyed with her dear Horace. What a wonderful husband he had been, so kind to her, so thoughtful all the days of his life.

Yes, Serena and Stephen needed that kind of simple affection. It would not hurt them, for she saw them both as disciplined individuals who would not allow themselves to fall in love, so what could be wrong with enjoying each other's company for the short while Serena would be there?

She drove Serena to church, refusing to get into Serena's sports car. "I need something more substantial between me and the car in front," she told the young woman. Serena smiled and teased, "I'm not going to have an accident, Miss Vivian."

"Of course you're not. But sometimes cars have minds of their own." They went in Miss Vivian's Lincoln that weighed over five thousand pounds.

Serena went to the Sunday school class for single adults and found a group of twenty-five men and women from their mid-twenties to their forties who came from various backgrounds and occupations. She wanted no special attention paid to her, but did not lie about her name either. Fortunately, the teacher simply welcomed her warmly and didn't make a fuss, and Serena was grateful.

She did, however, during the class notice stares coming from Mary Upton and her friend, the girl with the short, brown hair. Serena could not help but feel embarrassed that she had been seen kissing Steve in his office, and she wondered if Mary hoped to be Steve's wife. From the young woman's facial expression, she could read neither approval nor disapproval of her, but only curiosity.

She enjoyed the lesson, but hurried from the class as soon as it was over so she wouldn't have to talk with anyone. During the time between Sunday school and the morning worship service, she wandered around the church and through its several buildings. What she saw impressed her, for the facilities were neat and organized, and the people efficient in carrying out their responsibilities.

When she was walking by a classroom in the Youth Building, she discovered an amazing thing: there, alone in a room, a girl of eleven or twelve was sitting at a piano, plunking at the notes, obviously not knowing how to play but singing anyway.

This singing captured Serena's attention, for the young voice was exquisite. Untrained, of course, but with a rare quality that promised great talent.

Serena hovered at the door, watching the child. She was not dressed all that well and her dull brown hair hung down her back in a straight, unstylish clump.

"Serena? What are you doing here?"

Serena turned quickly and laid two fingers over Steve's mouth. "Who is that?" she asked in a whisper, nodding her head toward the young girl. The girl was still singing and playing in a haphazard way, unaware she was being watched.

Steve took Serena's arm and led her down the hall a ways.

"Her name is Jennie Blake. She lives with her grandmother. Both her parents are dead. Why do you ask?"

Steve was thrilled to see Serena there, pleased that she had chosen his church in which to worship, but her acute interest in the Blake girl mystified him until she eagerly explained.

"Just listen to her." Serena's fiery green eyes opened wide in some kind of excitement Steve could not fathom.

"All right, I hear her. She's playing around. So what?"

"She's talented, Steve, really talented," Serena insisted, clutching his arm. "Listen to the pitch, it's perfect. Hear how she runs up and down the scale with amazing clarity. She's a natural musician, and I really think she could be a brilliant vocalist if she were properly taught."

Steve shook his head sadly. "I doubt she will ever be able to afford lessons, Serena. Her grandmother receives only a small pension. They live in a poor neighborhood, and most of the money is spent on the necessities of food and clothing. I'm sure there would be not enough to pay for singing lessons."

Serena looked stricken. "Oh, that's terrible, Steve. That wonderful child has a rare gift that should be explored."

Steve was touched by Serena's compassion for this girl she did not know. To feel so deeply about a stranger was unusual, and was one more quality that Steve admired about Serena.

"I have to go," he said. "The service begins in five minutes."

"Oh, I'm sorry I held you up."

"I'm glad you did."

He wanted to kiss her, right there in the hallway, not caring who saw them. The inclination was so strong that Steve actually took a step toward her, but was stopped when a noisy group of junior high students burst into the hallway and crowded past them. The size of the group in the narrow confines of the hall forced Steve and Serena to huddle together against the wall, and his arm instinctively went around her waist to hold her up against the jostling flow of youngsters.

"Kids," Steve muttered fondly, but Serena shook her head back and forth.

"It's wonderful that they're here in church—and so enthused to be so."

Steve smiled in agreement. "I really must go. See you later."

"Oh?"

"Yes. Miss Vivian has invited me to Sunday dinner."

"Wonderful."

As Steve hurried away, Serena's mind flashed back through the years. How very often she had heard her mother say, "I've invited so-and-so for Sunday dinner." Rarely a week went by that a friend or stranger did not sit at the Lawrence family table, Serena remembered. She also remembered the delight in her mother's eyes as conversation flowed around the abundantly laden table, almost always, though, in the later years, to be followed by weariness from the effort of cooking and cleaning up.

Serena had helped as much as she could, and her father had urged her mother not to work so hard, but Millicent Lawrence could not stop caring for people just because she was tired. Even after she learned she had cancer, her house continued to be a haven for people of all sorts with varying needs.

A blur of movement caught Serena's eye, and she saw Jennie Blake leave the room in which she had been singing. She moved quickly along the hallway and up some stairs, and Serena followed her, not sure why, but wanting to be near her.

twelve

They emerged at the back of the sanctuary, and Jennie walked with head down, not greeting any friends, to the third pew from the back in the far right section. Serena carefully sat down beside her, but not too close, and noticed how eagerly the girl took a hymn book, opened it, and scanned the pages, stopping now and then to mouth the words of a particular song.

During the service Serena listened, enthralled, as Jennie sang heartily with the congregation, her young voice right on pitch, her rhythm perfect, her vitality apparent.

Something must be done to give that child a musical education, Serena thought, and she didn't stop pondering the situation until Steve began preaching. Then, her whole attention was riveted on the man standing beside, in front of, or near the pulpit—but only rarely behind it.

Steve was a restless speaker in that he moved a lot, his long, lanky body surging with energy across the platform, his enthusiasm reaching out to the people, capturing their interest and never letting it go. His deep, strong voice used the cordless lapel mike well, projecting into the farthest corners of the large sanctuary, his enunciation clear, his ability to hold the people to him in a room so large a credit to his "presence."

Serena knew this was his second service of the day, and every seat was taken. Miss Vivian had told her a third service might need to be added, or an expansion made to the church to accommodate the ever-increasing growth of worshippers.

Steve's natural, down-to-earth charisma was not the only thing that drew people there, Serena soon determined, but the common sense message he preached—a message filled with stories and anecdotes that illustrated the main point that he continually emphasized: "Being a strong Christian will give you the ability to meet any situation with hope, and enable you to overcome." He used as his text a verse Serena knew well—II Timothy 1:7: "For God has not given us a spirit of fear, but of power, and of love, and of a sound mind."

He spoke of a partnership with God, of drawing on His promise to be with us and carry us through any happening in our lives. "God is Lord of our circumstances," he insisted. "Look at Job, that magnificent man we read about in the oldest book in the Bible. Satan attacked him mercilessly, taking from him his children, his livelihood, his wealth, his health, and even the respect of his friends and wife." Steve's voice rang through the sanctuary, not so much with fiery oratory but with the firm, believable passion of a man who knew what he was talking about.

Most people there were aware of the personal tragedy in his life, and how he had courageously and successfully gone on with his responsibilities after the death of his young wife.

"Yes, Job lost everything but his unbendable faith in God. 'Though He slay me,' Job said, 'yet will I trust Him. . . . But as for me, I would seek God, and to God I would commit my cause, Who does great things, and unsearchable, marvelous things without number.'"

Steve's professional skill as a speaker was not what moved Serena's heart to tears, nor the logical elucidating of Biblical truth that forced her to admit she was living a life of fear because of the threat that hung over her voice, her career, her very joy of existence. No, it was the Spirit of God Who moved through Steve's words and thoughts, using him as a channel to speak to the people assembled there. Steve was God's mouth, and heart.

One could feel this pastor's love for his people, his sensitivity to their needs, his genuine caring that they learn to be strong, overcoming Christians.

Serena was more than blessed that morning, she was shaken from a destructive path of mental negativity. She prayed earnestly for God's wisdom, and forgiveness, through Jesus Christ, the first heart-to-heart conversation she had had with her Maker in too long a time. She prayed in full faith that from this day on, her life would be different, knowing this recommitment of her life to God was the first step.

The service ended, and Serena turned, intending to talk with Jennie Blake, but the girl was gone. *Just as well*, Serena thought. *What would I have said to her?—You are destined for great things if you are properly trained?*

She stayed sitting in the pew, waiting for Miss Vivian who had told her she would be a few minutes late for she had a brief meeting of some sort.

Serena felt a little guilty for not having sat with Miss Vivian, but when she had seen Jennie, and followed her to the sanctuary, she had totally forgotten about her hostess.

She watched the people filing out, young and old, men, women, and children. What was it about them that caught her attention? Ah, it was their smiles. They were a happy people, as Christians should be.

Serena bowed her head and began to pray, or rather to empty her mind and listen to what God would say to her. She needed His strength and wisdom to grow stronger, both in her spiritual life, and in facing the future with her voice.

She had no idea how long she sat there, with her eyes closed, but she felt the air move as someone sat down beside her. Expecting it to be Miss Vivian, she opened her eyes and was surprised to see that it was Steve.

The sanctuary was empty, except for a few members of the choir who were conversing in the loft.

"Are you all right, Serena?" he asked, concern coloring the words.

She looked at him, this wonderful, righteous man, and said, "Better than I've been for a long time, thank you."

"Oh?" He looked puzzled.

"This was a wonderful service today, and your sermon touched my heart."

"I'm glad."

She lowered her gaze to her lap, suddenly shy to share the decision she had made with him, but knowing she should witness to it, for then it would be stronger.

"I'm back, Steve."

"Back?"

"With the Lord. Wholly. Committed. I never stopped believing, but I allowed other things and attitudes to choke my growth."

She looked up into his compassionate eyes. "Will you pray for me? There are two things in my life that are of great concern to me—one from my past, and the other in my future."

Steve nodded. "Of course I will, if you'll do the same for me. People often think ministers have all the answers and no problems, but they're wrong. We, more than anyone, need the prayers of the saints. Will you do that for me, Serena?"

"Yes, of course."

Their eyes stayed on each other and Serena knew she was in the presence of God's man. Steve was dynamic and successful, but humble, a man who simply wanted to be God's instrument. This moment, when their souls touched, profoundly moved Serena to an even greater determination to live her life for the Lord.

"There you are." Miss Vivian's voice came from the back of the sanctuary to break the mood. "Are you ready to go home?" she asked Serena.

"I am home," Serena said softly, and Steve heard her and understood.

Serena went back to Steve's church the next Sunday, and returned for the Wednesday night Bible study. She was an eager pupil and sat in the second row.

During choir practice, she moved to the last pew so she could observe unobtrusively, and when the director, a man of considerable girth who was about her own age, asked her to sing with them, she declined sweetly, but asked if she might be allowed to stay and listen. Of course, the answer was yes.

Serena went with Miss Vivian to her next daytime Bible study, and it happened the teacher was sick. When the group asked if anyone could teach that day's lesson, Serena volunteered, as the passage was one she knew well and had, in fact, taught before.

The women were blessed and enlightened by her intelligent but down-to-earth instruction, and duly reported to Pastor Shepherd her ability.

Naturally Steve saw Serena at church, and they began going out for coffee, or he'd drop in at Miss Vivian's and they'd spend time together. Neither of them were ready to call it dating, but they also didn't know what they should call this growing relationship.

Serena wondered if anyone at the church noticed the time they spent together, and whether they cared. Walter Thomas did, she felt, for he was less than cordial to her, and the last time she spoke with him, he asked her when she was going back to New York. She told him after the concert, June 24th. He seemed relieved to hear that, but even saying the words made her sad. She did not want to leave Steve.

Then, one night before Bible study, while she was praying in the small chapel off the sanctuary, she overheard a disturbing conversation. Two women were talking, and Serena soon realized the voices belonged to Mary Upton and her friend, Judith, both of whom she had spoken to several times.

While both young women had been friendly to her, Mary was more so, genuinely interested in her career, Serena thought, and a nice person. *Steve could do worse than marry her,* she had thought at the time, for Mary was personable, articulate though soft-spoken, and possessed a certain dignity which would only be enhanced with age.

"I don't know what he sees in her," Judith said. "She's a celebrity and. . .and a Yankee. She doesn't belong here."

"She's beautiful and talented and is an interesting person," Mary defended her. "I've spoken with her several times and. . .like her."

"Steve does too. Isn't that the problem? He should be liking you. You're perfect for him. You're both from old Southern families and understand each other's world."

"That world is changing, though, Judith. It seems half the people we know now are from the North, or the West. Anyway, our similar backgrounds isn't reason enough for Steve to fall in love with me."

"But it's a good place to start—*if* you didn't have competition from that. . .opera woman. I hear that her father has some business in Pennsylvania, in Gettysburg, no less. Imagine."

Serena bemoaned the fact that only one door led out of the chapel, and the two women were right outside it; otherwise she would have escaped and listened to them no more. She had her answer to a question she had been pondering: Is Mary Upton interested in Steve? The answer was yes.

In the weeks she had been coming to the church, she had only seen Steve and Mary together once, and while Steve had been cordial, he had not shown more than a pastor's interest in the woman. Of course, they could have been together at other times Serena did not know about.

The real question was, Could Steve develop feelings for Mary if she, Serena, were not in the picture? Was it fair of Serena to take up his time, because in all honesty, most of the hours they spent together now had nothing to do with the Arts Council or her upcoming concert.

Selfishly, she was enjoying Steve's company, and knew he cared for her, as she did him, even though they both knew their relationship would end the day after the concert, when she returned to New York.

Do I really want it to end? she asked herself now, rising from her knees while Judith and Mary continued to talk outside the chapel door. *Can I give Steve up? Is my singing more important than a life of love with a wonderful man?*

"Once she leaves here," Judith was saying, "Steve will see that you are the perfect woman for him, Mary. I know he will."

Serena heard no more conversation, and she assumed they had moved on. Trembling, she sat down on a narrow pew and buried her face in her hands. *What should I do with my life, Lord? Are you trying to tell me something and I'm just not listening? I leave it in Your hands.*

She sat there, waiting for God to speak to her, until she heard people gathering for the Bible study. When she went to join them, she still did not have her answer, but she did have peace in her heart that God's Holy Spirit would guide her.

thirteen

The idyllic weeks of spring in the South drifted by. The azaleas bloomed and died. Green and prolific kudzu, a rampant ground cover with huge leaves, flourished in every neglected field and ran rampant up trees and poles and along the ground, swallowing up whatever lay in its path; when the weather was exceptionally hot, it could grow an entire foot in a day. The whippoorwills sang their nesting call far into the night, and lightning bugs danced silent through the darkness, the delight of every child who tried to catch them in old Mason jars.

Plans for the concert continued on schedule. Tickets were nearly sold out the first week they were available. Radio, television, and newspaper interviews went well. Serena had suggested the Graylin Symphony Orchestra accompany her for four numbers and a local pianist of fine reputation, Daniel Jerrod, for six more. Her program was a short one, but she had decided she would be wiser to be conservative than risk damaging her voice. To make the entire production longer she had asked the orchestra to do several major numbers alone, and the conductor and musicians were thrilled.

Serena worked with the pianist once a week for just an hour. Fortunately, Daniel was a superb technician who knew the numbers she had selected and was amazingly intuitive to exactly how she wanted them presented. Their rehearsals together were productive and pleasant, and, most important, not tiring to Serena's voice.

She determined not to practice with the orchestra until the day before the concert, leaving the conductor to bring his musicians to a fine level of interpretation.

Serena now faced her uncertain future with optimism, but still did not share her health problems with either Miss Vivian or Steve, for she did not want them to be concerned about a "possibility."

Miss Vivian taught her to cook a few Southern dishes: barbecue pork, Brunswick stew, fried chicken, catfish, green beans cooked for hours with bacon and onion, skillet corn bread, sweet potatoes, and Steve's favorite, pecan pie.

She also taught Serena to recognize the different hummingbirds that inhabited the garden, pointed out the distinctive bleep of the invisible, tiny tree frogs, and explained her name—Vivian Barnsley Hall.

"Southerners are interested in bloodlines and believe in giving names to their children that remind them from whom they came. Often, a family's last name will become a child's first name, especially if there are only girls to carry on.

"My actual name is Barnsley Vivian Hall—Barnsley is from my mother's side. She was related to a wealthy cotton merchant who built an impressive mansion and estate for his Savannah bride in northwest Georgia. And Hall is from my father's side. His ancestor was one of three Georgians who signed the Declaration of Independence."

Miss Vivian sighed. "As you can see, though, I decided that being addressed as Vivian suited me better than Barnsley, so I unofficially changed the order."

Serena's eyes, wide open in interest at this piece of Southern tradition, held a sparkle as she realized Miss Vivian was a spunky lady who liked doing things her way.

Steve came early one evening and declared, "We're going out on Lake Lanier in my boat. I don't know why I haven't shown you the lake before now."

"Sounds like fun," Serena exclaimed. "It's big, isn't it?"

"Six hundred and seven miles of shoreline."

"Wonderful. Let me go get Miss Vivian."

Steve caught her arm as she rushed past him. "No Miss Vivian."

Serena looked up at him in question.

"Tonight, Serena, I want it to be just you and me."

His husky voice conveyed the same emotion she, herself, was feeling. They needed to be alone. They were ready for whatever the next step in their relationship would be.

"All right," Serena said quietly.

"Great." Steve kissed her cheek tenderly, slowly, his nearness sending her pulse racing. "Fishing on Lake Lanier, and you. An unbeatable combination for a balmy spring evening."

"Wait a minute," Serena cried, punching him playfully on the arm, "who said anything about fishing? I want a tour of the lake, the homes around it."

"Which you'll get while I'm trolling—

"Trolling?"

"Moving slowly with a line in the water."

"But I want to go fast."

Steve chuckled. "There are times to go fast and times to go slow. This is definitely a slooooow night."

"Fast."

"Slow. It's my boat."

Serena glared at him and plopped both arms across her chest. "I'm not going."

Steve grinned. "On your own two feet or over my shoulder,

you're going. It's your choice."

They walked out of Miss Vivian's house laughing, both of them imagining what Miss Vivian would think were she to see Steve marching down the sidewalk with Serena over his shoulder.

The night was perfect to be on the lake. The sky was cloudless and the temperature hovered around eighty degrees. Steve's boat, a 16-foot blue and white bowrider, could seat eight, and Serena sat in every seat before deciding she liked the front best, with her legs stretched out in front of her, the wind whipping through her hair as Steve plunged the boat through the water at a speed she definitely called fast.

He also fished, around the docks and brush piles by the banks, and she was amazed at his ability to find an endless supply of three-pound bass that took his spinner bait with relish. The smaller fish he released back into the lake, but the bigger ones he attached to a stringer and left them in the water, to be taken home, and eventually eaten.

"If you're especially nice to me, I just may barbecue one of these for you some day," he promised Serena.

She gave him a saucy look and replied, "What do I have to do to be nice to you?"

Steve cut the engine and left his seat to come up to Serena's. Kneeling on the floor of the boat, he slipped his arms around her waist. "Just this, Serena," and he kissed her long and well.

The boat bobbed at anchor while Serena read a novel she'd found in Miss Vivian's library and Steve fished. Sometimes they talked with each other, but for long stretches there was silence as both enjoyed what they were doing, an enjoyment heightened by having each other nearby.

The sun had nearly set, and Serena sighed and stared out across the water. The sun was a huge ball of fire, its orange splendor dancing off the water in liquid pools of beauty as the quiet of the night closed in around them. The time had come to tell Steve about her mother.

"She was a wonderful woman," Serena began her account, after Steve had put his fishing gear away and she had tucked her book safely in a tote bag, "kind, sensitive, always ready to go the second mile for someone who needed help." She couldn't keep the awe she had always felt for her mother from sounding in her voice. "She died when I was fourteen."

"A hard time for a young girl to lose her mother," Steve commented sympathetically.

Serena nodded. "I was devastated—and angry."

"Angry?"

"Because she was so busy with her church work she didn't have time to see a doctor."

Steve frowned. "Did she tell you that?"

"Yes. Oh, I know she meant to go. She wasn't afraid of doctors, but there was always one reason after another that kept her from taking care of herself instead of all those others."

Serena paused, feeling the same bitterness rise to her throat and knowing it had no place in her newly committed life. She had to let it go.

"I stopped going to church after that," she went on. "For six months nothing my father said could convince me to go."

"Because you blamed the church for taking away your mother?"

"And God. I was angry with all the people who had used the last drop of my mother's energy, and angry with

God for assuring her that what she was doing was good and noble." Her eyes flashed. "But it wasn't good. And it wasn't fair. I needed her. My father needed her. If she was doing such fine things, why was she taken away? Why wasn't she allowed to do more? Why does God always require more than we have to give?"

"He never does that," Steve said gently. "He always gives us the grace and ability to carry out His work. Your mother was open to Him, and was an exceptional woman."

Serena sat up so suddenly she rocked the boat. "A foolish woman, and one who cared about other people more than she cared about her own family."

"Do you really believe that?"

"I have for almost twenty years."

Steve reached across the aisle and took her hands. He waited until she was looking at him, searching for answers in the depth of his eyes, and then he said, "Your mother lived her life for others, and I know, I am certain, you were more important than anyone to her."

"No, you don't know that," Serena argued in a small, child-like voice. She fought the tears that welled up in her eyes and felt the ache in her stomach that had lived there for so long.

"Serena, your mother may have been wrong in the amount of time she gave to the church. Even fine, selfless people misinterpret God's will and let their misunderstanding lead them to make unwise use of their time."

His words, meant to comfort Serena, jolted Steve's awareness that he, too, had been guilty of that error. Wanting to serve God to the best of his ability, he had neglected his young wife.

He leaned forward and brushed away a tear that had slipped onto Serena's cheek. *She's hurting. How can I*

*take away that unhappiness? I want to hold her. Just hold
her.*

He knew that if they were on land now instead of in the
boat, that's exactly what he would do. Take her in his
arms. Comfort her. Tell her. . . .

"I know my mother loved me, Steve, and I also know
I'm probably wrong in judging that others meant more to
her than Dad and me. I said before that I didn't go to
church for six months after she died, but by then I knew
that I missed that time of worship. I missed my friends. I
felt . . . empty, as though it had been a long time since I
had eaten a proper meal.

"I had given up reading my Bible, too, and one day I
looked at it, lying dust-covered on my nightstand, and I
started to cry. I grabbed it up, and hugged it to me, and
just held it for the longest time, knowing I needed its
wisdom and understanding. I needed God's very Word to
get me on with my life.

"So," she smiled, and the light that came on in her eyes
sent a rush of relief through Steve, "I started in the Psalms
and read all 150 chapters before I put it down."

He laughed, and Serena grinned. "I got involved again
in my church, but then, as I was building my career, I
slipped away as time became more precious and I gave
up one activity and then another. I always told myself I
would go back, but I didn't."

She smiled broadly and grasped Steve's hands. "That
Sunday morning not long ago, I made the journey, in your
church." Her eyes filled with tears. "Thank you for being
the instrument to bring me back."

Steve felt a tear or two in his eyes, too, and silently
thanked God for Serena's reawakening. She was a strong
woman, a woman of courage. A woman with questions,

but aware of where the answers lay—in God. She was
. . . an exceptional woman, and one he cared for more
than he should.

Back at the marina, Steve guided the boat into slip 41
and turned off the motor. Hopping off the front of the
boat, he securely tied the bow line to a metal cleat, then
turned to help Serena ashore. He held her hand as she
stepped on the seat and then onto the rickety wooden dock
which moved, making her stumble. Steve's arms shot
around her and pulled her against him.

"Oh," she cried.

"You're all right." His voice was deep beside her ear. "I
have you."

The words wended their way through Serena's heart
and she thought how wonderful it would be to be his. To
have such a strong man beside her, a man she respected
and trusted. A hard-working man. A man who was good
and fun to be with, a man who could make her tremble
with a glance or a touch, as Steve was doing now.

"Thank you," she murmured, wondering why, oh why,
with all the men of her acquaintance throughout the world,
was she so attracted to this particular one? Serena was
afraid to lift her head for fear he'd kiss her, even though
what she most wanted was for him to do just that.

"Are you okay now?" he asked softly.

"Yes, I'm fine." She wasn't fine. His arms were still
around her, and her heart was racing at a frightening speed.

"I need to tie down the boat," he said.

"Of course."

"Do you want to help?"

"How?"

"By. . . ." He leaned back and looked down at her. "By
. . . ." Then his head lowered and she was lost in the rich

sound of his voice, the hunger in his eyes. "By . . . kissing me," he said so softly she thought she had misunderstood him.

But there was no misunderstanding the strength of the arms that pulled her close, or the desire in his mouth as he claimed hers with a fervor that buckled her knees.

"Serena." He whispered her name as though it were a symphony, and Serena responded by twining her arms around his waist and returning his kiss with ever-increasing passion. She was filled with joy, and longing, and she knew, from the urgent way he held her, he had not kissed a woman for a long time, not the way he was kissing her now.

Their lips parted, but they remained together, their foreheads touching, their arms still around each other.

"That made the day complete," Steve said, shaken by how much he wanted to go on holding her.

"For me, too," Serena answered.

"Thanks for coming out with me."

"I wanted to. It was all that I'd hoped it would be."

He kissed her again, lightly, dwelling on her lips, savoring them and the magic of the moment.

"What's happening with us, Serena?"

She nestled against him. "I'm not sure, but it's wonderful."

"Yes." The physical touching and his basic need for a woman were not what made him feel it was Christmas morning and all was right with the world. Down deep it was a feeling of completeness, a wholeness that comes from finding that certain person who walks in your rhythm. Serena was that person, or seemed to be, even though the rational side of him insisted she could not be.

He secured the boat in four more places, Serena

eagerly receiving his instructions on how to tie the ropes to the cleats. "How'd I do, Captain?" she asked, her face flushed and her eyes dancing.

Steve ruffled her thick, disheveled hair. "Fantastic, mate."

Their eyes met, and held. *Take her home NOW*, a warning message pulsed in his brain, and he did, but he held her hand in the car, and they shared more of their lives and laughed together. At Miss Vivian's front door, Steve kissed her again and promised to call her the next day.

He drove home in a fog, his heart near to euphoria. "I don't know why you've brought Serena Lawrence into my life, Lord," he prayed out loud, "but even for this brief time we've had together, I thank you. I'm a new man."

fourteen

The next Saturday, Steve was hurrying past some of the Sunday school rooms, when he heard a piano playing and a young female voice singing. Then an older woman's voice began instruction.

He walked into the room and was surprised to see Serena sitting on a piano bench with Jennie Blake, the young girl whose voice had so impressed her.

"Open your mouth wide, Jennie, and let the sound out. See? Isn't that better? Richer?"

Steve listened, unobserved, for a few minutes, then left the two girls alone.

Later, though, he found Serena before she went home and invited her to his house that night for barbecue. "Do you want some of the bass I caught or hamburgers? The extent of my culinary talent is grilling fish and hamburgers, maybe hot dogs, too, and slicing watermelon," he told her. "If you want baked beans and cole slaw, they have to come from a nearby deli."

"I'll pick them up," she said, anxious to see his house and to be with him.

"Great, then come at seven. Miss Vivian will give you directions."

They walked slowly out the front door of the church to Serena's car, and kissed lightly before she got in and drove away.

This was the first time Serena had seen Steve's house. It was a nice-sized brick home, set on a large grassy lot punctuated by pines and dogwoods and a few crepe myrtle bushes that would soon be in bloom.

Inside, the two-story had three bedrooms, two baths, an attic, and a study, all the rooms filled with comfortable, if not stylish, furniture and a lot of light from the wide windows.

Steve's favorite room was, of course, his study, where he had a big desk, lots of bookshelves, and a mammoth, well-used recliner that sat in front of a 36-inch television. "I love sports," he explained. "The big screen was a birthday present to myself." He beamed, proud of his purchase.

Serena's favorite room was the sun porch which overlooked the backyard and a stand of slender Georgia pines. Beneath them, nestled in an island of pine straw, bloomed a dozen or so brilliant lavender irises.

While the coals got hot on the grill, they sat talking, she on a white, wicker chair, and Steve on a long, wicker chaise. Closing her eyes, Serena sighed, "I could stay here forever." She listened to the sounds of the neighborhood— the barking of a dog next door, some children laughing down the street.

Steve kicked his shoes off the end of the chaise and asked, "How was your interview yesterday for the local paper? Did the reporter get to Miss Vivian's on time?"

"On the dot. I gave her a few of my press releases so she could choose which best suited this area, and she asked a few questions. I don't think she knew much about music, so the interview was short."

"When is it due out in the paper?"

"Next Wednesday, I believe."

"Did she take pictures?"

"A half dozen or so. She didn't want any of my professional ones. How was your day?"

As Steve answered, he couldn't help thinking how special this time was, relaxing together on the porch, not in a rush to do anything else, but able to enjoy each other's company. *This is what marriage should be: sharing. Caring about each other's important and unimportant events of the day.*

He swallowed hard, knowing he was living a brief dream with Serena, making a memory that would last him a lifetime. He would always be grateful for it.

"I saw you with Jennie Blake today," he said. "It sounded to me as though you were giving her voice lessons."

"I am," Serena confirmed with great enthusiasm. "She's going to meet me at the church twice a week. Oh, Steve, she has such natural ability."

He looked at her seriously. "Do you really think giving her lessons is a good idea?"

Serena missed the less-than-enthusiastic tone of Steve's voice. "Yes, of course, it is," she bubbled. "It would be a crime not to bring out such talent."

"Can you do that in just a few weeks?"

Serena laughed lightly. "I'm afraid not."

"Then what will happen to Jennie when you go on with your career?" Steve asked. "Aren't you teasing her unnecessarily?"

Serena stared at him and frowned. "You honestly don't approve of my helping Jennie, do you?"

"No, I don't."

Serena took a quick breath and let it out. "That poor child needs to know she has talent."

"Then what?"

"Someone must teach her."

"Who? Do you know a teacher who will do that for nothing?"

"I will."

Steve suddenly stood up. "You will only be here a little while longer, Serena. When you go, what happens to Jennie?" His eyes were dark. "You're thinking of yourself, not her. You're having a good time, but Jennie now sees herself as someone special. When that 'specialness' is taken away, she'll be devastated."

Serena was stunned by Steve's negative reaction to her teaching Jennie. How could he not see how excited she was to be helping someone else to develop a talent like hers? And she had no intention of abandoning the child once she left; she'd find someone else to teach her. But who?

"What about Randall Dawson, your minister of music? Maybe he could continue the lessons when I'm gone," Serena suggested, as the idea came to her. "He seems very capable."

Steve shook his head and guided Serena to the backyard, where he put a half dozen hamburgers on the grill as well as some fish wrapped in foil. "Between directing a forty-voice sanctuary choir, overseeing the youth choir, putting on two major cantatas a year to which the community-at-large is invited, selecting and rehearsing special music for two services every Sunday, Randall has all he can handle."

"But she's just one little girl."

"All right, let's say Randall agrees to teach her. Then Susie Doe learns of the free lessons and wants them, too? And Dick Jones, and Benjamin Miller?"

Serena's mouth tightened. He was jumping to the conclusion that the scenario had no positive solution, but it did.

"It would be nice if the church could give free music

lessons to everyone who wanted them or deserved them,"
Steve went on, sounding like a father scolding his child,
"but it cannot. There is neither the time nor the staff, let
alone the money."

Serena was crushed. Her discovery of Jennie, and desire to teach her had given her great joy. Now Steve was
destroying that joy. "Are you forbidding me to work with
Jennie?" she asked. There was a stubborn tilt to her chin.

"Forbid is a strong word," Steve responded. "Discour-
age would be better, especially if you continue to do it at
the church. Now, if you work with her somewhere else, I
have no authority to tell you what to do."

Serena's temper rose. She had been a star long enough
to be used to people doing exactly as she wished. She was
not at all happy that this bossy minister was telling her
not to do something she very much wanted to do.

"Please take me home," she demanded.

"Serena, the hamburgers are almost done."

"I'm not hungry."

Steve put down the spatula he'd been using, and faced
her. "Can you see my side of it?" he asked, wanting to
repair the breach.

Serena walked quickly back into the house and picked
up her purse. "Certainly," she answered without looking
at him, "but I'm disappointed you think so little of my
intelligence to assume I would raise that child's awareness and then abandon her with it. I would have found her
another teacher. There must be someone capable in town
since your minister of music is far too busy."

The truth was, though, she'd been so caught up in "dis-
covering" Jennie that she *hadn't* looked beyond her own
involvement with her, although she certainly would have,
in time. She would never admit that, though, to Mr.

High-and-Mighty.

In his position, no doubt he was used to having the last word, just as she usually did in hers. The fact that they had finally tangled over an issue that each felt right about was probably inevitable. The problem would be solved easily enough if Serena could find a suitable teacher, but could she find one in this small town who would teach the girl for nothing? Times were tough, and music teachers needed to make money just like everyone else.

The galling thing was that Steve had not trusted her to handle the matter properly. That was what hurt. She wondered if he were one of those men who doubted women had a brain in their heads.

"Serena," Steve pleaded, "please come back and eat. We'll agree to disagree on this one, and talk of something else."

Reluctantly, Serena changed her mind and stayed, but the evening was ruined, their conversation stilted.

When Steve took her home, she couldn't bring herself to get into a cheerful mood, and when she thanked him for the meal, her words were flat.

All the way to Miss Vivian's, Steve wondered how he could have better presented his views on the subject of Jennie Blake. He knew Serena was put out with him, and he was sorry for that, but he was concerned with Jennie, swept into a new and exciting world by a beautiful lady who was rich and famous and promised her a future the girl would never have dreamed of before.

His lack of trust in Serena's judgment was what was bothering her, he knew, and he also saw the temper of a celebrity used to having her own way. That attitude would never work in local church life where people had to work together and prima donnas created problems. Not, of course, that that would ever be the case with Serena. In three more weeks she would give her concert, receive the accolades of a grateful Graylin and Hall County, and then be on her way to New York, or Paris, or Vienna, to pick up her glamorous life. She would leave behind pleasant memories—and an aching heart for him.

They reached Miss Vivian's, and Serena darted out of the car without waiting for Steve to come around and open the door for her. He caught up with her on the front walk and took her arm, holding it firmly when she tried to pull away.

"I'm sorry if I hurt your feelings, Serena. I didn't mean to offend you by not trusting your judgment."

He turned her to face him, both hands on her shoulders. "Don't let this ruin our friendship. I know you would never intentionally hurt Jennie."

"No, I wouldn't," Serena retorted. The stab of guilt she felt at not admitting she had not thought the situation through softened her anger. "I do understand, though, your wanting to protect Jennie from disappointment."

She looked into his eyes to see if the closeness they shared had disappeared, and her heart skipped some beats when Steve slowly smiled, activating those adorable dimples of his.

"Then we agree the important thing here is Jennie?"

"Of course."

He drew her into his arms and she rested her head against his shoulder, her cheek feeling the soft fabric of his chambray shirt.

"Why don't you go ahead and teach her," he said, "and we'll work together to find her a replacement teacher when you go." He kissed her forehead. "Not that anyone could ever replace you." He kissed both cheeks. "Because you are one of a kind, Serena Lawrence."

He kissed her mouth and Serena responded. The fervor of his embrace and the sound of his quickened breathing was matched by Serena, and she melted against him, relishing the exhilaration of being in his arms again, where she knew she belonged.

They said good-night and both were glad they had not ended the evening with the quarrel still between them.

fifteen

Steve was moody at times. He didn't realize it, but his secretary did, and his assistant pastor did, and the director of women's ministries did, and Walter Thomas, head of the deacon board did, as did Randall Dawson, minister of music.

"Who's put the burr under the pastor's saddle?" they asked each other, none of them realizing that Steve's testiness was growing worse the closer the time came to Serena's concert.

He thought more and more about this Serena Lawrence who had swept into his church and had everyone goggle-eyed over her. She was an excellent communicator, was compassionate and understanding, and had a real gift for putting people at ease and assuring them she cared about them. Through a sincere interest in their lives, she won friends at every turn.

One person who particularly enjoyed the friendship of Serena was the church's minister of music. Whenever Randall Dawson spoke of Serena, a telling glaze came over his eyes, and his voice softened and seemed to caress every spoken thought of her. He was so obviously star-struck that Steve had at first dismissed it as meaningless. Lately, though, he felt irritated whenever he saw Randall and Serena talking together.

Ordinarily, he would have been happy for his minister of music, having the opportunity to share thoughts with one of the major musicians of the world. He had deduced, however, that Randall had a distinct liking for Serena that went beyond her being an outstanding singer, and he was no longer quite as happy for the man.

The longer Serena was there at the church—and she came Sunday mornings and Sunday nights, and to the Wednesday evening prayer meeting and Bible study, as well as to the women's Bible study—the more Steve heard of her many virtues.

"I wish she were going to stay in town," Margaret Smythe, director of women's ministries, told Steve once. "She's an excellent Bible teacher, and we could certainly use her for one of our home study groups."

"Miss Lawrence is so sweet," Sally Griffin, Steve's secretary told him. "She brought me a box of candy for my birthday. My favorites, too. How did she know?"

"She's going to donate some classical records to our church library," Virginia Hobson, the librarian, informed Steve.

"The Senior Citizens love her. . . ."

"She spoke last night to the teenagers about priorities— spiritual versus secular. . . ."

Miss Vivian, of course, seldom let a day go by without praising Serena, then there was Jennie's grandmother who came to Steve's office to give him her thanks for letting Jennie take lessons at the church, and Jennie herself who had miraculously blossomed and matured in the few short weeks since Serena had been working with her.

Serena seemed to be everywhere in his church, adding converts to her fan club daily, all of whom were vocal in praise of her, to the point that Steve was made even more aware of how his congregation needed a pastor's wife. Obviously, Serena would be perfect in that role—except that Serena Lawrence was not an ordinary woman who was free to fall in love with the pastor and marry him, no matter how happy that might make the church, not to mention the pastor himself.

Oh no, Serena Lawrence was a dream, a sweet, sweet dream that was about to end.

One Friday night he had just watched the evening news while eating leftovers, and was on his way to his study to review his sermon for Sunday, when the doorbell rang.

His heart leapt when he saw Serena. As usual, she was beautiful in a pistachio linen pantsuit, her hair tucked behind her ears, her eyes dancing with life. She smelled wonderful, or was it what she was carrying?

"Come in, come in," he invited her, hastily tucking the tail of his yellow knit shirt into the waist of his bluejeans.

She extended toward him a pie covered loosely with saran wrap. His mouth watered when he saw it was pecan, his favorite. *Miss Vivian must have made it*, he thought, noting the perfectly fluted pastry and the crusty brown top laden with pecan halves.

"I hope you'll like it. I just made it, and it's still warm," Serena surprised him by saying. "It's my very first attempt. Miss Vivian gave me her favorite recipe."

Steve took the warm dish from her, knowing it was going to be delicious. Their fingers touched as they exchanged the pie, and the softness of her hands holding such a wonderful gift alerted Steve that he was in trouble: he could not resist Serena Lawrence any more than the people of his congregation.

In the kitchen, Serena said, "Why don't I cut us both a piece and we can talk, if you have the time. I hope I'm not interrupting."

"No, not at all," Steve assured her, forgetting the

sermon he'd been about to review, thinking only of the warmth of her eyes and the smile that made him glad he was not going to spend the evening alone.

He was home very little, actually, partly because he was busy and partly because it was too quiet a place, too filled with unsettling memories of Stacia.

"Oh, no," he heard Serena cry out, and he followed her gaze to the counter where another pie lay, another pecan pie with two slices missing. Two very large slices.

"Someone else brought you a pie," she said, crestfallen, and he could have kicked himself to next Thursday for not putting away the pie when he'd finished with it.

"Yours will be twice as good," he assured her, putting hers down on the counter and clumsily slipping some foil over the culprit pie which he threw rather than placed in the refrigerator.

"Did you just have some?" Serena asked, her eyes filled with disappointment that her surprise was diminished in her own eyes, though certainly not in his.

"A small piece," he told her. "A very small piece."

"There are two pieces missing, and they aren't small."

"I've had the pie for awhile."

"Who brought it?"

"That isn't important. I know your pie will be wonderful." He gave her an encouraging smile.

"Who brought it, Steve?"

His eyes flew around the kitchen. Was it ever right for a minister to tell a white lie to keep someone from feeling bad? No.

"Mary Upton."

Serena's mouth dropped open. "Mary was here?"

"She bakes a lot."

"For you?"

"For . . . everyone, actually. She's a gourmet cook."

Serena groaned and picked up her pie. "I'll just take this back home. Miss Vivian will like it."

Steve snatched the dish from her hands and plunked it down on the counter.

"If you made this for me, Serena Lawrence, then it will stay with me. I want it." His eyes softened. "You were an angel to make it for me."

He swept her into his arms, and kissed her, hoping to assure her that anything she brought him was highly prized, as she was herself. Looking down at her after a few moments of savoring the sweetness of her lips, he said, his voice low, "I'm glad you came by. This is a different house with you in it."

Serena allowed a smile to tug the corners of her mouth upward. "I like being here, Steve. I think you know that."

"And do you like the owner of the house, too?" His voice was almost a whisper.

Serena broke away from him and cast a playful glance at him. "I may like the owner of this house if he eats a huge piece of *my* pecan pie."

They laughed together and Steve cut them both big pieces. They carried them out to the sun porch where Serena sat in the same chair she had used on her last visit. Steve again relaxed his tall body onto the chaise.

"It's cool here," Serena sighed.

"Thankfully. Last year at this time we were sweltering with daily temperatures in the nineties that lasted into the nights."

They ate quietly and Steve groaned in honest appreciation of the taffy-sweet flavor of the pecan delight.

"Do you really like it," Serena asked, "or are you just pretending?"

Steve gave her a thoughtful look even as he took another big forkful and said, "I'm not sure. I may have to have another piece before I make up my mind."

Serena giggled. "Thank you."

They ate slowly, listening to the night sounds of cicadas presenting their never-ending symphony and watching the fireflies flitting just beyond the screen of the porch. "This is so peaceful," Serena said with a sigh. "If I lived here, I would never leave this porch."

Steve's heart lurched. If she lived here. . .if he could come home and find her on this porch, eating pecan pie, the smell of its baking fresh in the kitchen. . .if she were his. . . .

sixteen

Serena put her plate down on a small wicker table and turned to Steve. "I came by for another reason than to deliver the pie. I want to talk with you about an idea I have for the church. I've already discussed it with Randall and he thinks it's great. We hope you'll agree."

Steve carefully speared with his fork the last sweet piece of filling. He tried not to visualize Serena and Randall excited over a project they no doubt had already spent considerable time on. If he gave his approval for this project, no doubt they would work together even more in the future. "Tell me about it," he said, with nominal interest.

"Well, Randall and I think there should be a music school connected to the church."

"Connected?"

"Taking place within, would be a better choice of words." Serena's eyes shone with enthusiasm. "The thought came to me because of Jennie, and the realization that there are probably lots of children who have musical ability—which the church needs in its ministry—but who will never have a chance to explore that ability. We can teach them voice, instrumental—"

"We?"

"The church, of course."

"The church."

"Randall said he can find teachers—"

"And these teachers will be paid?"

"A small fee for those who cannot afford to donate their time."

"So these lessons will cost money?"

"If the family can pay. If not, then the lessons will be free."

Steve let out a big sigh, seeing the problems, and surprised that Randall and Serena had not seen them, too.

"Won't that kind of inequity create friction between those who have to pay and those who don't?"

"It would all be confidential. No one would know. Payment would be based on ability to pay."

"The church, then, would pick up the extra cost for instruments, music, stands, paper—"

"No."

"No?"

Serena shifted uneasily in her chair and looked out at the yard. Why was she afraid to say it? Why did she feel as though he did not like the idea already? They had been so relaxed, being here alone together like this. She didn't want it to change. "I will pay for it," she took the plunge and said.

Steve grunted in surprise and swung his legs off the chaise and onto the floor. Leaning forward, his arms resting on his knees, he looked at her with incredulity. "*You* will? You've got to be joking."

Fiery green eyes pierced him. "Certainly not. I know the church doesn't have that kind of money. Perhaps someday the school will become a paying institution, but for now I'm very willing to underwrite it."

"As long as it carries your name?"

Serena's mouth dropped open. "Do you honestly think that's why I'm doing this—for publicity?" Her heart fell to the floor. *How can he think that of me? Why isn't he caught up in the greatness of the idea, as Randall was?*

Steve sat up straight. "I wish you had come to me with this first."

"First?"

"Before talking with Randall about it."

Serena's eyes narrowed. "Is this a question of authority, Steve? Yours over Randall's? You're the senior pastor? He just works for you?"

Steve stood up abruptly. "Now just one minute," he exclaimed. "I don't have an ego problem, Serena, but I do have responsibility to a lot of people, and that means analyzing a project very carefully before committing the church to it. Anyway, aren't you getting a little too involved in this congregation? In another two weeks you'll be gone. What about the church and Jennie, then?"

Serena stood and faced him, her heart pounding in her chest. She had not been looking for unadulterated praise, but neither had she expected his opposition. She honestly felt the Lord was laying on her heart to give back to Him some of what she'd received.

"Speaking of Jennie," she went on, trying to keep her voice level, "I've found a wonderful teacher for her when I leave, a woman who used to teach at Julliard, where I studied. She left the school and moved here with her husband when he became ill and needed a warmer climate. She teaches a few select young people now, and was happy to add Jennie to that group, on my recommendation."

"Are you going to pay for those lessons, too?"

"Yes." Her eyes narrowed as she prepared for another negative reaction from him. "I can't walk away from Jennie and leave unfinished what I've started. She's become precious to me, Steve. Her talent must be brought out, and I can well afford to pay for the lessons."

Steve flung his hands up in the air. "Are you trying to buy your way into heaven, Serena?"

Serena gasped. "How can you say that? I've been a born-again Christian for a long time. I got off the track for some years, but being here, with these wonderful people, with. . . ." She stopped. She'd been going to say, "with you," but now could not. "I've made a fresh commitment to the Lord, Pastor Shepherd, you know that, and I'm trying to do what I believe God wants me to do."

Steve slowly shook his head no. "Your heart may be in the right place now, Serena," he said in a tone of voice that irritated her because it sounded like a professor scolding a student, and he'd used the word "may" which meant he doubted her commitment, "but it would be a big mistake to take on either project you've just told me about. What you do with Jennie, of course, is your own business, but what you want to do in the church is mine, and I can't approve it. I won't."

Serena's cheeks reddened in frustration. "How can it be a mistake to help children discover their talents?"

He faced her squarely. "How many years did you take lessons, Serena? How much training did it take to get you where you are today, as well as money? Are you willing to take on that much responsibility with Jennie, and with any number of other kids, or will you forget about them all in a year or two when you are busy with your own career, jetting all over the world? Two years from now, five years from now, will you still remember the little girl in Graylin, Georgia, to whom you gave a dream that some-day she could be a great singer?"

He reached out and took her hands, which were cold and trembling. "I know you are a caring person, but in Jennie's case, and the other children you say you want to help, I honestly believe it is a misplaced caring."

Serena felt as though she had been kicked in the stomach. What had made her feel so good, so happy, was turning into a condemnation on her motives and herself as a person.

Quietly, barely in control, she faced him and said, "I can't believe you're questioning my intentions. You make me sound like a pampered star who enjoys throwing her fame and money around without regard to who gets hurt." Her eyes narrowed. "I got where I am today, Steve Shepherd, by being focused and determined. I have a reputation in my world of always following through on my word. If I say I'm going to sing, then I sing. And if I say I will support those children in a musical education, then, with the help of God, I shall do just that."

She scooped up her purse and strode off the porch, through the living room, and was at the front door before Steve caught up with her.

"Serena, I'm sorry. It's obvious I've misjudged you. Forgive me."

She looked into his eyes and saw repentance there, but that did not take away the hurt that somewhere in his mind he doubted her sincerity. Oh, he could apologize, but the thought was there, and she realized she could never live up to his image of what a Christian woman should be. He saw her only as someone desirous of pleasing herself, a self-centered star used to getting her own way, a woman clever at bringing attention to herself.

"Serena," he said gently, taking her hand, "let's talk about this some more."

She swallowed, near tears. This man had spoiled a lovely dream, for the church and for them as a couple.

"Another time, perhaps. I really must go."

She pulled her hand from his and was out the door but then turned around. "I hope you enjoy Mary Upton's pie!" She threw the words at him, then hurried to her car even though he called her name over and over.

Why, why, why, did I ever let him into my heart? she railed at herself, and when she got into the car, she slammed the door and squealed the tires as she drove away.

seventeen

The night of the concert, Serena was nervous. She knew most of the audience would be surprised to know that, for many people thought a professional singer, after hundreds of concert appearances, no longer felt anxiety before a performance. But she did; she felt it all—a sick feeling in the pit of her stomach, moist palms, a restlessness and anxiety that was heightened by not being able to remember the very first word she was going to have to sing.

She was always nervous, to some degree, every time she sang, but it went away just moments after the first notes were sung. Then she relaxed and enjoyed the thrill of performing some of the greatest music ever written.

Tonight, she was more anxious than usual because of the condition of her voice. To protect it, she had had to practice far less than she was used to, which meant it was weak, like an unused muscle. Extreme self-criticism during practices with the orchestra and the pianist had told her she would have to be very attentive to every note.

She wanted to give a stellar performance for these people, because they deserved it, and she was a professional who tried never to give less than her best. Every person she had worked with on the concert had been gracious and helpful; just because Graylin was a small town compared with Atlanta or New York or Paris, did not mean excellent musicians would not be at the concert, people with trained ears and knowledgeable in the music she was to sing. For them, and for everyone who had paid money to hear her and support the drive to build a performing arts center, she wanted to be outstanding.

"Oh, dear Lord," Serena prayed, sitting at her dressing table backstage, "please help me through this tonight. Give me strength where I have none. In Jesus' name, I pray."

A knock on the door interrupted her thoughts, and when she went to answer it, Miss Vivian stood there, a dazzling smile on her face, her eyes dancing with excitement.

"I can't believe this night has come," she said. She swept into the room and gave Serena a hug, which Serena returned.

"You look beautiful," Serena said to her, and she did, a picture of elegance in a gown of electric blue, complemented by a choker of cultured pearls and matching teardrop earrings, gifts from her late husband.

"I'm here to help, my dear," she told Serena.

"Which I can use as I'm about to get into my dress." Serena had almost called her longtime companion, Deborah, to come and be with her, but had decided not to at the last moment, still hoping to keep her condition secret from everyone but her doctor. If anyone could discern her voice was not up to par, Deborah would be the one.

From the closet, Serena pulled an ivory satin hanger on which hung a peach-colored gown she had found in an exclusive shop in Atlanta just the week before. Whirling it through the air, the skirt billowed outward, showing its design and flair. Miss Vivian gasped.

"How very beautiful," she exclaimed, "as you will be in it." Her eyes enfolded this young woman of whom she had become so fond.

Miss Vivian unzipped it down the back, and Serena stepped into the shimmering creation. She stood still in front of the mirror while Miss Vivian closed the zipper. The material floated over her figure, drifting over her hips and legs to the tops of her matching low-heeled shoes.

The color of the dress complemented her auburn hair hanging long and full around her shoulders. An eighteen karat gold flower pin with matching ear-clips completed her attire.

She thought of the outrageous price she had paid for the jewelry, as she did all her jewelry, and thought of how Steve had questioned her willingness to pay for Jennie's vocal lessons for as long as she needed them. He had probably thought it would cost too much money over the years to make such a commitment, but that, for her, was not a problem. Between her singing engagements, recording contract, and product endorsements, she was a wealthy woman who handled her money wisely, saving as much as she spent. Steve should not have worried that she could not afford to help a child who needed it.

Steve.

She had not seen him for two weeks, since the night at his house when they had disagreed so sharply over her involvement in the church and Jennie. He had called her several times and left messages for her to call back, but she hadn't. He'd come to Miss Vivian's once, but she'd been gone, and he'd left her a note asking her to contact him. She hadn't.

Her heart ached because he had not trusted her common sense where Jennie and the music school were concerned, and because he'd doubted her recommitment to God. She knew she'd been temperamental, not making an effort to see him again and resolve the bad feelings, but every time she'd been about to contact him, she'd thought, *What's the use? My time here is almost finished.*

It's just succumbing to the temptation to be with him, and there's no future to it except a bruised heart.

The hectic schedule of final preparations for the concert had drawn her mind away from Steve for hours at a time. But when she had found herself alone at Miss Vivian's, the urge to call him had been almost overpowering.

Several times she had actually had the phone in her hand, but then had put it down. What would she say to him? Should she apologize—but for what? Hadn't he made it perfectly clear he did not want her in his life, or in the life of his congregation?

Looking at herself in the mirror now, she saw an attractive, successful woman. She had everything she'd always wanted. Even her relationship with God was back where it should be—centerstage.

Then why do I feel so miserable? she thought. She knew why, though; tears sprang to her eyes at the thought that she might never see Steve Shepherd again. Miss Vivian had told her someone else would be driving her to the airport the next day.

Maybe he won't even be here tonight. He probably doesn't want to hear me sing. He's probably eating something else at this very moment that Mary Upton's baked for him. Is he with Mary Upton?

There was a knock on the door and Miss Vivian went to answer it.

Steve.

Serena saw him in the mirror, behind her, tall and urbane in a black tuxedo with satin lapels, so handsome, so desirable. In his hands he held a dozen yellow roses.

She turned, and their eyes met, his serious but filled with the same longing she knew was reflected in her own.

She wanted to run to him, throw her arms around him, and tell him she loved him and did not want to leave him, ever.

Just a few feet separated them, just a few feet to his arms, those strong arms that had held her in a world like no other she had ever experienced. Her legs wouldn't move, though; she was too overwhelmed with the fact that he was even there, extending toward her a bouquet of flowers—a peace offering?—a declaration of love?

"I must see to something," Miss Vivian said, and hurried out the door, leaving them alone.

When they heard the door click, Steve crossed the room to her and threw the flowers on a nearby chair. Roughly, he pulled her into his arms, his kiss sudden, and passionate, possessing. Serena's head was dizzy from the power of him, but her own pent-up desire for him rushed forward, and she wrapped her arms around his neck and gave herself to their embrace.

"Serena, Serena," he crooned her name, and lavished her face with kisses. "I had to come." His voice broke. "I love you so much, and I didn't know what to do about it. Everyone in the church adores you and that only made me feel that much worse that soon you were going to be gone. I wanted you to stay, not just for them, but for me. For me, Serena."

He took a deep breath and pulled her into his arms again, and she rested her cheek against his while her heart throbbed in turmoil. She could hardly believe that he loved her. He loved her.

Steve stepped back and ran the back of two fingers over her lips and down her throat. "I know you love the Lord, Serena, and I understand that He's calling you to use your unique abilities for Him."

She smiled up at him. "I do, and you can trust my motives in wanting to help your people."

He kissed her gently. "The truth is, I don't want to give you up—to your career, and to the rest of the world who can't possibly need you as much as we do, all of us, my people. As much as I do!"

He kissed her slowly and with great tenderness, so that Serena could barely stand when the last touch of his lips left hers. He smiled, just a little, just enough for those adorable dimples to emerge. "Have I made a total fool of myself—again?"

She gazed into his eyes, and let out a long, deep sigh. "You are . . . you are the most marvelous, most lovable man, Stephen Shepherd. I would have died if you hadn't come tonight. I felt so awful, that I had done something to upset you so. I thought you might be with Mary Upton."

"Mary?" He looked puzzled.

"She would make a wonderful wife for you, wouldn't she?"

"No."

"She's from a fine, old Southern family."

"I don't care."

"I think she likes you, and Walter Thomas thinks you should marry her—" She began to sniffle.

"Sh, sh," he comforted her. His hands took hers and kissed separately each and every finger. "I don't want Mary Upton. I have never wanted Mary Upton. I don't care if Walter Thomas wants me to marry Mary Upton. I want you, Serena, as I have from the first moment I saw you on that stage in Atlanta. I love you, my darling."

Miss Vivian came back into the room, saw the discarded roses lying on the chair, saw Serena's hair disheveled and her lipstick smeared, and said, "Good heavens, my dear, what happened to you?"

"Me," Steve responded forcefully, his smile broad, and proud, like a predatory animal who has just staked out his territory. Then he and Serena both laughed, and she picked up the flowers and buried her face in them. Miss Vivian clucked her tongue and said, "You only have ten minutes until you are to be on stage, Miss Lawrence. Shall we repair the damage?"

"Damage?" Steve questioned, giving Miss Vivian a wink. "You're too big a man for me to physically throw out of this dressing room by myself, Stephen," she responded, "so I'm asking you to leave. Now."

With a twinkle in his eye, Steve grabbed Miss Vivian around the waist and twirled her in a circle. She gasped. "Let me down, you beast."

"Yes, ma'am," he said obediently, setting her gently on her feet and giving her a quick kiss on the cheek. "Take care of my girl for me."

Miss Vivian snorted, "Your girl?" She gave a sharp look at Serena, but she and Steve were already kissing again, and Miss Vivian took the roses and said, "Not that anyone cares that these poor darlings are crushed and starving for water, but I shall try to do something about that. Stephen Shepherd, leave!"

Steve stood with his arms around Serena's waist. "I'd better go." He kissed the tip of her nose. "After the concert, we'll talk. Really talk."

He left, and Serena felt like bursting into song right then. She had never been so happy, so eager for another day. For a brief moment she forgot the cloud that hung over her, the threat, and she went on stage and sang as she had never sung before.

eighteen

The concert was glorious. The orchestra performed Tchaikovsky's *Pathetique* Symphony, Liszt's *A Faust* Symphony, and other pieces with great precision and transparency. Their immaculate intonation and commendable balances made Steve proud of them, as he was of Serena's performance.

He sat in awe at the display of her magnificent lyrical voice with its amazing purity and shimmering clearness. Her phenomenal talent enabled her to offset delicate pianissimo phrases with dashing forte climaxes, to soar effortlessly to the highest coloratura range, then almost weep through a poignant rendition of the spiritual, "He's Got the Whole World in His Hands."

She was a presence—exuding radiant innocence and captivating charm that caused one adoring fan to cry out during a silence between numbers, "Miss Lawrence, we love you."

An easy thing to do, Steve agreed, as he watched and admired this woman he had held in his arms just moments before. He had told her he loved her. He'd wanted her to know that before going on stage, wanted her to know that even though they had disagreed over the music school and Jennie, she still owned his heart.

Now, though, he wondered if he should have confessed his love for her. How he felt would not give them a future together. That was impossible. Saying good-bye now would only be that much harder.

For one glorious moment, though, just before the concert, they had been united in their passion for each other. Oh yes, she'd felt it, too, he knew, had wanted his arms around her and his kiss as much as he'd wanted them.

That memory will have to last me a lifetime, he thought sadly.

The concert was longer than expected, four encores following Serena's stirring presentations of Bizet, Purcell, Schumann Lieder, Mozart, and Richard Strauss. During her second encore number Steve noticed the change—in her voice, and in Serena's concentration. She was...struggling. Why? Those compelling green eyes he knew so well, that usually held a vibrant enthusiasm for life, were fatigued, stressed, the energy lacking from her body as though all life had suddenly been drained.

The audience did not seem to notice, but Steve knew something was seriously wrong, and the moment the conductor made the last cutoff on the last encore, Steve vaulted from his seat and raced backstage, past dark-clothed orchestra members and local dignitaries, electricians, and crew. He had to get to Serena. He was scared.

A quick knock at the door and he burst into her dressing room. She was sitting on the sofa, leaning forward, a handkerchief over her mouth, her body a picture of exhaustion.

"Darling," he rushed to her and dropped to one knee, "you were magnificent. There aren't words to describe—"

He stopped, appalled at the paleness of her face and the nearly hysterical look in her eyes as she lifted them to his.

"What's the matter?" he asked, grasping her hands, terrified at the gasp of agony that escaped her mouth. The handkerchief she clutched told the story—it was stained with blood. Her blood. He could see a tiny drop of it on the side of her lips.

"Serena!"

She collapsed in his arms.

Steve paced the floor of the hospital, refusing to sit down even at the urging of Miss Vivian.

"She'll be all right," his friend promised him, but he was filled with doubt.

"How can she be all right when she might have cancer?" He sobbed and hit the wall in front of him with the palm of his hand. "Cancer! In that incredible voice."

"*Might* have cancer, Stephen. The doctor doesn't know yet."

He whirled around and fixed Miss Vivian with a frightening stare. "Why didn't she tell us? Either of us? Why did she go on with the concert knowing something was wrong with her throat?"

Miss Vivian shrugged her narrow shoulders and looked down at the floor, fighting back tears of her own. She did not know the answer to that question. She had thought she and Serena had shared a warm relationship. Why had the girl not confided her condition to her? Why had she taken such a risk?

"Serena will tell us when the operation is over, Stephen, when she is better."

"*If* she gets better."

"She *will* be all right, my dear. You are praying for her, I am praying, as is your whole congregation. I called her name in to the prayer chain."

Steve hardly heard what she said, his heart was in such distress for what Serena was going through, at that very moment—doctors probing, cutting—and he was powerless to help.

"Singer's nodes," the doctor told Serena, "is what you have. They are thickened or swollen enlargements of tissue on the vocal cord. In your case, they were on the top and sides of the cord. The bleeding was caused by a leaking blood vessel."

Tears rushed down Serena's cheeks. Dr. Bradley, a young man about her age with unruly dark hair and a no-nonsense demeanor, pushed his glasses further up on his long, crooked nose, and said, "These seldom are cancerous, Miss Lawrence, but we've sent a biopsy to the lab to be sure. Frankly, it was a miracle that you were able to sing at all. The nodes were very hard, and would not have gone away by themselves. You had to have surgery."

Serena scribbled a word—PROGNOSIS?—on a pad of paper. She had been ordered not to speak. *Will I ever be able to sing again?* she thought desperately.

The doctor pulled up a chair beside her bed. They were in a private room, small and dimly lit. "I wish I could guarantee that your voice will be like it was before," he said, "but I can't. You may get it all back, or you may get only half. You may lose your top register. You may be able to sing, but it's not likely to the level you need to perform in opera."

He gave her a sympathetic look. "I wish I could be more encouraging."

Serena tried to smile her appreciation for all his effort on her behalf, but it was too hard to do so. She was still groggy from the anesthesia, but awake enough to know that God had not answered her prayer. For months she had "reminded" Him that she needed to be healed. She had begged Him. More than once.

Why was she here? She believed in spiritual healing. She believed God wanted her well, not. . .damaged.

"You must be totally quiet for two weeks," the doctor instructed her. "*Very* limited speaking for another week, absolutely no whispering, then restricted speaking for another two months. If all looks well then, you will be allowed to begin limited vocalizing, but you must be cautious and not push. Warming up the voice will be vitally important in any singing you do." He smiled, for the first time since he'd been there. "But, of course, as an outstanding vocalist, you know that already."

Serena silently nodded her head to show she understood. She wondered if her own doctor, Dr. Jeffries, would agree with this man's conclusions.

"There are two people waiting to see you," Dr. Bradley told her. "Can I trust you not to try to speak with them?"

Serena shook her head no, and turned on her side. She did not want to see anyone, not even Steve and Miss Vivian. She did not want their pity.

"I'll explain your situation to your friends," the doctor said, and left the room.

Serena stared at the wall, void of hope. Her world was gone. She knew she would never sing again, at least not in opera; the demands on the voice were too great, and she would not risk humiliation by trying to sing again and failing to live up to her former ability.

The silence in the room contributed to her drowsiness, and she continued to weep as she drifted toward sleep, feeling cold, her last thought of Steve and how she wished his arms were around her. Then she would be warm, but she would not be singing.

nineteen

After two days in the hospital, Serena went to Miss Vivian's to recuperate and rested there another few days until the biopsy report came back: benign. She did not have cancer.

Steve came to see her every day, but of course she could not talk with him. She communicated by writing on a pad of paper, and what she wrote this particular day ripped through him like a blow to the stomach: "I'm going back to New York to recuperate."

He had thought she would stay there, with Miss Vivian, at least for a few weeks, but no, she was leaving, in less than an hour.

"You need to be with people who care about you," he said gently. "Miss Vivian wants to help you. I want to." He meant it. He knew he should let her go, but he couldn't. Some voice in his head kept telling him to hang on to her.

He stared at Serena, sitting on an upholstered chair in Miss Vivian's living room, dressed in khaki-colored summer slacks and a matching short-sleeved blouse, her suitcases around her on the floor. Her face was deceptively calm, her expressive hands controlled as she wrote. If someone did not know her the way he did, they would think nothing was wrong with her.

He knew her too well, though. She was in denial, still in shock. Since the operation, she had not cried once in front of him, never bemoaning the cruelty of what had happened to her. She had not condemned life, or Satan, or anyone.

She was just . . . quiet, changed . . . patient with his and

Miss Vivian's eagerness to help, but closed off. She wasn't
there any more. Her spirit had slid into a world of, what?
Self pity? Defeat? Resignation? Steve didn't know,
because it was hard to convey deep feelings through notes
on a piece of paper, and that was the only way he and
Serena could communicate.

She handed him the note. "You both are very kind, but
I don't need to be taken care of. I'm fine. My father is
coming from Pennsylvania, and I'll have my friend,
Deborah."

"But I want to be there, too, Serena."

She shook her head no.

"I'm sure I can help in some way. Don't shut me out. I
have some vacation time coming—"

Serena laid her hand on his arm and silently mouthed
the word NO.

Steve was not a man who liked emotional scenes, but
right now he would give anything if Serena would get
angry, yell, cry, throw something. She needed to do that—
and pray. Had she prayed, to the God she had so recently
returned to? Had she felt His love, and remembered that
He would walk with her through the dark valleys to come?

She was writing again. "There is much business to attend to: engagements to cancel, etc. I can only do that at
home, alone."

"Will you at least write?" he asked her.

She frowned and mouthed the word "maybe," and Steve
knew she wanted to put him out of her life. Whatever she
was going to do in the future would not include him.

He longed to take her in his arms and assure her
everything would be all right, would be like it was
before, her career intact, she still a diva of world renown
for many years to come. He longed to do that, but knew
he couldn't. The fact was, her life would never be the
same again. The doctor did not know how long the

healing would take, or if the healing would even be complete. Serena faced months of uncertainty, a career shattered, probably never to be regained.

He, too, faced a loss that tore at his insides: he loved her, and wanted her in his life, but she was leaving him, bringing reality to the fact that she never could have been a small town minister's wife.

Wife?

Oh yes, he sighed, gazing at her these last few minutes together, memorizing the lift of her brows, the curve of her mouth. More than once he had daydreamed what it would be like to be married to her.

Serena had made him realize just how lonely he was without a Christian woman to share his life and his ministry. He had thought his work serving God was enough— but it wasn't. He needed someone beside him. God had known that man would need a soulmate as far back as the Garden of Eden. That's why He made Eve for Adam.

Serena was his Eve. She was all he had ever wanted in a wife: loving, intelligent, genuine, compassionate, and most of all, a child of God, and growing more spiritually mature daily.

If he were married to her, he would not make the same mistakes he had with Stacia, neglecting her, being insensitive to her needs. He had honestly thought he would never love again, but he was loving Serena, and felt more strongly with each day that God had had a part in bringing her to him.

He took Serena's hands and helped her to her feet, then smiled as best he could, wondering what she'd do if he asked her to marry him, right then.

"I'm going to miss you," he said, knowing that was all he could say, and that it was the understatement of the year. "Your being here has changed my life."

His right hand reached out to gently touch a soft curl

that lay by her ear. "Oh, Serena," he whispered, and he pulled her into his arms and buried his face in the sweet, fragrant mass of hair that covered her neck.

He held her, wanting her to feel his strength, to use it as her own. Her perfume filled his nostrils, the soft, gauzy fabric of her blouse was nice to touch. Silently he thanked her for giving him new life, for opening his heart to manly feelings he had not enjoyed for far too long.

He held her, and waited for her to respond, but she did not. Her arms were loose around his waist. She was not the same woman who had clung to him with passion just before her concert. That woman of vitality and excitement was gone, perhaps forever.

He stepped back and gazed at her lovely face, trying to find the words to say good-bye, the words she needed to encourage her, the words to tell her how much she had meant to him and the people of his church these past few months. He should have been able to express the feelings in his heart, but he couldn't. The words would not come— the words that would tell her he loved her, that he wanted her in his life forever.

"I wish I were driving you to the airport," he finally managed to say, and with a slight wave of the hand and a lifeless smile, she conveyed to him that she didn't mind that he wasn't.

He wanted to kiss her, but he didn't.

He wanted to laugh and hear her laugh. He wanted to promise to pick her up that night and they'd go out on the boat. He wanted to give her roses. He wanted—

"Good-bye, Serena." He swallowed hard. "I'll never forget you."

He walked away from her then, and she didn't run after him, or try to stop him. She let him go, and in his car, he wept—for both of them.

Serena watched Steve walk away from her and knew

she would never get over the pain of leaving him. Perhaps she had been cruel not to encourage him to come and visit her in New York, but what would be the point?

She could have stayed there, in Graylin, to recuperate. Her agent could have come there and they could have worked together to straighten out her threatened career, but Serena did not want to impose any more on sweet Miss Vivian, especially since she knew she was not going to be her best for several months. She knew she was going to feel sorry for herself for awhile, and pout, and try to fix blame on everything but the real culprit: life, just plain life.

She had never liked that Bible verse that said the rain falls on the just and on the unjust. She had always wanted to believe that when one was a Christian, one's life would be perfect, without heartache or problems.

God had never promised that, though, and she knew that, in her head, but her heart was frustrated with Him for not somehow saving her from what she was now going through.

Why, Lord, didn't you heal me? she had asked a dozen times while lying alone in the hospital before and after the surgery. *There are verses that say You heal, that promise recovery. What did I do wrong not to receive Your blessing? I know I should be positive, and concentrate on what I have and not what I've lost, but that's hard to do.*

She was going back to New York because she didn't want Steve and Miss Vivian to see the confused, bitter woman she was at the moment. She couldn't have faced watching their opinion of her change, especially not Steve. Leaving him was the bitterest pill of all to swallow, but she'd had to do it. Her life was a shambles. Until she knew who she was and what she was going to do with herself for the rest of her days, there was no room for a dynamic, young minister who had captured her heart.

He had told her he loved her, before the concert. Those words, so precious, had also scared her. *Where does he expect this love to take us?* she had wondered, while walking the long, dimly-lit corridor to the stage. *Does he want me to give up opera and marry him, and live here in Graylin?*

At that moment, the idea had appealed to her strongly, and it had given her an incredible energy to get through the concert. Even as she was singing, she had been thinking of Steve, and what it would like to live with him for a lifetime, loving him and sharing his ministry, dreaming with him and planning their days and having his children and growing old with someone who would love her with a Godly love.

That was all a woman could ask or hope for, but was it meant for her? How could it be, when she'd worked so long and hard to get where she was? Was she to give it all up, for love?

She'd almost decided to leave her profession to become Steve's wife—until the concert had ended, and her throat had bled.

She was glad she had never told Steve she loved him, although surely he must know she did. Still, she could leave him more easily because they had no commitment between them.

Now it was time to go.

Miss Vivian wept and held Serena in her arms like a mother. "Please call or write me whenever you need someone to talk to," she urged.

Serena wrote her, "You are a special woman, dearest Vivian. I can never thank you enough for all you've done for me."

Serena was grateful that the Assistant Director of the Arts Council talked continually during the fifty-three mile drive to Atlanta. The endless conversation helped Serena not to think of what she was leaving, what she was choosing to give up. Circumstances had not forced this pain upon her; she had made her own conscious choice, and she would have to live with that choice forever.

twenty

The next month was a painful one emotionally for Serena, letting friends know what had happened to her, canceling contracts and appearances through her agent.

The people in England were devastated that she would not appear in *Madama Butterfly*, and insisted on rescheduling the opera for the following season, despite being told she might not regain her voice even by then.

This was a dark time for Serena, a spiritual valley. The recommitment of her life to God while at Steve's church had given her such happiness and hope, a hope which had been dashed with her surgery.

She did not believe God had made this terrible thing happen to her to punish her, but He *had* allowed it to occur, and she thought she should "feel" His presence more than she did. She thought that through prayer she would know for a certainty what His plan for her was. But she didn't know. Was He not hearing her prayers?

She felt lost, adrift, and question after question poured through her mind at all hours of the day and night, questions about her physical condition, her future, about Steve and why he had become a part of her life.

Deborah was staying with her in New York and was a great comfort to Serena. Deborah rode Serena's ups and downs day after day, allowing her to express her thoughts without judgment. Deborah's compassion, though, was tempered with doses of realism.

"Honey," she said to Serena, "change comes to all of us

at one time or another in our lives. Sometimes we want it; sometimes we don't. It's how we handle that change that makes us a winner or a loser."

"You're right," Serena agreed, knowing it was her choice whether she was master of her problem, or it mastered her. "It's just that for so long my life has been focused on opera, it's overwhelming to think of doing anything else with the same passion."

"Let's pray you won't have to." Deborah looked Serena straight in the eyes. "But if you must, you must." She took a long sip from the iced tea she was holding and asked, "What would you like to do if you weren't performing?"

"Teach." Serena was surprised at how quickly the answer sped from her mouth.

"Any number of fine schools would scramble to get you on their faculty," Deborah said.

Serena nodded, knowing that her success could open many doors other than performing. "I think, though, that I would prefer teaching privately. Working one-on-one with individuals would be most satisfying."

Immediately, the expectant face of Jennie Blake leapt into her mind, and Serena knew, in that instant, that she could have great joy sharing her education and experience with someone else.

"I don't want to be pessimistic, though," she said to Deborah. "My voice may be fine. I could be back on stage before the year is out." She ignored the small voice in her head that asked, *Is that even what you really want?*

Serena spent hours reading her Bible, staring out the window of her New York apartment at Central Park. Day or night, the view, for which she had paid handsomely, blurred into an indistinct tapestry of green trees, city sidewalks and streetlights, and gray, blue, or black skies.

Having always been a decisive person, she was used to making things happen, right away. Now, though, she was having to learn patience, for God's answer did not come in a thunderbolt, and she waited, knowing she did not fully understand His ways.

After the first two weeks of total restriction of speaking were over, her father came and stayed with her. They had a good time together, though Serena spoke as little as possible, as advised by both Dr. Bradley and her own Dr. Jeffries.

Mr. Lawrence was a young-looking 62, with still-thick hair, the color of Serena's, though sprinkled with gray. His eyes were the same vibrant jade green, and his mouth generous and usually turned up in a smile—again, like his daughter's.

They shared a sense of humor, and keen intelligence, but John Lawrence did not have an artist's soul. He was a businessman through and through, a problem solver, an unemotional, practical man who enjoyed working alone.

During this visit, Serena realized how much like him she was in some ways—tireless in pursuit of a goal, energetic, straightforward—but also like her mother—sensitive, intuitive of others' needs, capable of great emotion.

Their father-daughter relationship had always been strong, but this meeting added a new dimension; they became friends, for they shared their deepest feelings, and Serena felt comfortable asking a question that had been burning in her mind for a very long time: "Daddy, why did mother spend so much time at the church?"

A year ago she would have added, "Didn't she realize you and I needed her, too?" Now, though, her search for the truth was different because she had experienced the deep satisfaction of being part of a loving church family. She, too, had wanted to be involved in various activities, to see people she liked, but also to give of her abilities to help the work of the Lord. Through her involvement in Steve's church, she was beginning to understand her mother's motivation, if not her wisdom, in spending an excessive amount of time there.

"Honey," her father answered, "your mother had a gift for helping others, and she found it difficult to say no to people when they needed her. Remember that you were busy with your lessons and school. I was deeply involved in building up the business, so your mother had time on her hands. She felt that time was best spent serving God in whatever way she could."

Serena stared at a picture of her mother she was holding in her hands. Her mother was laughing, her arms around Serena's waist. Happy times. They had had many of those. "But, Daddy, why didn't she go to the doctor sooner when she started feeling ill?"

Mr. Lawrence shrugged his narrow shoulders. "I've asked myself the same question, Serena. I knew she was feeling poorly, yet I didn't insist she go. I left it up to her to do so. I was probably wrong in that, but I certainly don't blame the church for what happened. Your mother just did not make the wisest choice, and when she did finally get to the doctor, the cancer in her body was too far along.

"Believe me, Serena, she was devastated by that, not so much because of what it would mean to her, but because it meant leaving you and me."

He put his arms around Serena. "She loved us both very much. Don't ever doubt that."

Serena felt his tears on her cheek.

That night, in bed, in the quiet of the night, Serena read again the last letter her mother had written her. "My darling daughter," it said, "you are so very special to me, and

I'm sorry to have to leave you before you're grown. I would have loved knowing you as a woman. I am sure whatever you do with your life, it will include serving our great and wondrous God. Always put Him first, always, then all other good things will come to you."

The letter went on, but Serena did not see the words, for her eyes were filled with tears. She knew she had inherited from her mother a passion for life, a dedication to always do one's best.

Still, there has to be a balance, she thought, *and if God ever gives me a family of my own, I will know He wants me to spend as much time with them as I can while still serving Him, too. It is possible to do both, wisely.*

If God ever gave her a family of her own. . . .

The thought hung in Serena's mind. Children. She had always assumed she would, one day, have them, but with her career in constant motion, she had hardly stopped to realize that she was now in her thirties, and if she was going to have a child, she would have to do it soon.

Of course, one needed a husband first.

Steve.

Her mind raced through a dozen remembrances of Steve and things they had done together. She missed him frightfully, and longed to call him every day, but didn't because she wouldn't know what to say to him except, "I love you."

She admired so much about him: his calling, his leadership and intelligence, his sense of fun—not to mention his handsome looks and his voice that sent chills down her spine.

What is he doing this very minute? she thought, looking over at the clock on her nightstand. Eleven thirty. *Is he sleeping? Studying? At a hospital comforting someone? Maybe he's with Mary Upton, eating pie.*

She was suddenly filled with such a sense of urgency to hear his voice, to hear him speak her name, that her hand was actually on the telephone before she realized what she was doing. She sighed and withdrew her hand.

"Oh, Steve," she sobbed, "you'll never know what those few months with you meant."

She saw his face, the dimples, his eyes laughing, his mouth smiling. She saw his long, lean body loping through the halls of his church, or leaning against a wall in Miss Vivian's house, or sprawling on a bench in the garden gazebo. What an amazing, unique man he was, tucked away in a small town, and in her memory, forever.

The phone rang, and she jumped, startled from her thoughts. Quickly she picked it up before it woke her father.

"Serena?"

"Yes?"

"It's Steve."

twenty-one

Serena's breath caught in her throat. Did God hear and answer prayers even before one prayed them?

"Steve." She said his name as though it were the most precious name in the world. And it was.

"Did I wake you?" he asked.

"No, I was just lying here . . . thinking."

"About what?"

She hesitated. "Everything."

There was a long silence on his end of the line, then he said, "How is your throat? Healing okay?"

"I think so. No problems. I go to the doctor again next week. I've been very good, and have obeyed his orders explicitly."

"That's my girl."

Serena's heart stopped beating. *Oh, that I were your girl, Steve,* she longed to say. Hearing his voice only made her realize afresh how much she wanted, needed, to be with him.

"I've been praying for your recovery," he said softly, "and for you personally, that you'll be able to get through this without bitterness and will know God's will for your life."

"Thank you, Steve. I've been praying for you and your church."

"Really?" He sounded pleased.

"Yes. How is Jennie?"

"Enjoying her new voice coach; practicing faithfully."

"Miss Vivian?"

"Fit and feisty as ever. She misses you. Says her gazebo does, too, wondering where that soft-spoken beauty is that used to loll about in it and read out loud."

Serena laughed, though she shouldn't have. "Oh, Steve, it is so very good to hear your voice."

"I can come—"

"No, not yet. Maybe later."

"I don't want to wait."

Serena put her hand over her mouth so he wouldn't hear the difficulty she was having breathing. She would give a king's ransom right now to be in his arms, to be surrounded by his strength.

"Steve, please, I need time to sort things out in my life."

"I'm sorry, love," he said, "forgive me for being impatient. I'm not doing well since you left. My life is in black and white; with you it was living color, every time we were together. I miss you, Serena. I want to be there with you, to comfort you . . . ."

"I know. I know."

The silence lasted a long time, but it was sweet to Serena, because she could, in her mind, visualize Steve's broad hand holding the receiver, his eyes bright with love, as she knew hers were. She could feel his pain at their being separated, because it was her own.

"I must say goodnight," she said. "If I don't, I'll be tempted to talk too much."

"Okay. Just remember, Serena, that there are a lot of people in this little town in northeast Georgia who love you, and one man in particular. We're always here for you."

"I know. And Steve?"

"Yes, love?"

"Don't give up on me."

She heard a little gasp from him. "I won't, Serena. Never."

They said a hushed good-bye and Serena heard the click as the connection was broken. She turned off the light on her nightstand and slid beneath the sheets of her bed, staring ahead into the darkness.

Lying there, she spoke out loud to her Heavenly Father, as though He were sitting in a chair beside her bed just as her earthly father would. She told Him all the thoughts that were churning through her mind and shared ideas with Him. She knew He already knew what was in her heart, but it was pleasant to do so, to treat Him like a valued Confidante.

Suddenly she sat up and exclaimed. "I understand, Lord. Here I've been waiting until I had the feeling that You were close to me, that You were hearing my prayers, when the truth is that You are always with me, always listening, whether I feel it or not.

"If I'm pliant to Your will, Your Holy Spirit will guide me on the right path, even though I might not understand that leading, even though it might seem You are saying no to something I wanted."

She sank back against the headboard and smiled so broadly her mouth almost hurt. "Having faith means acting on that faith, no matter what the circumstances, no matter what I'm feeling," she said out loud. She reached for her Bible on the nightstand and opened it to a passage she had read just the night before, from Psalms 50.

The fifteenth verse gave the words of God: "Call upon Me in the day of trouble; I will deliver you, and you shall glorify Me."

The truth of the verse was clear to her. "I have called

upon You, oh Lord," she told Him, "and I know You will deliver me. Even though I don't understand why You didn't heal me so I wouldn't need surgery, I know whatever happens will be for my best. Please show me how I can glorify You."

A tremendous sigh escaped her, and then she remembered what her mother had often said in her childhood: "God said it. I believe it. That settles it."

Serena's heart was light, full of assurance that her future was indeed in God's hands, now that she had freely given it to Him, and she fell asleep almost before she finished thanking Him for opening her mind.

"Don't you dare tell Steve I'm here," Serena threatened Miss Vivian when she picked her up at Hartsfield International Airport in Atlanta, seven months after her surgery. "I want to surprise him."

Miss Vivian had been ecstatic when she'd received Serena's call that she was returning to Graylin.

"Are you totally well, my dear?" she had asked on the phone.

"Yes, Vivian, totally, thanks to the doctor's expertise, and God's wonderful healing. I'm whole again."

"When will you go back on stage?"

Serena had laughed. "I'll tell you all about it when I get to Graylin."

Now she was here, riding along the same tree-lined freeway she had traveled less than a year before with a tall, handsome minister who happened to be a music lover. She smiled; that minister soon had the surprise of his life coming.

The sky was overcast and a bite was in the air. The oaks along the freeway had lost their leaves, and the kudzu was brown and dormant, but the pines were still green as were most of the rolling hills they drove beside. To Serena, it was a most beautiful land, always alive with the promise of spring and the rebirth of all God's creation.

She hoped Steve would be glad to see her. They had spoken several times on the telephone in the early months of her recovery, and Steve had come to New York for a few days. They had had a glorious time together, and it had been as though they'd never been apart, so comfortable were they together, but Serena had still been healing, both physically and emotionally. She had not yet made her decision to spend the rest of her life with him.

After his visit, because she was still struggling with what to do with her life, she was not quick to respond to his letters, or phone calls, and eventually he stopped trying to reach her.

Would he want to see her now, or had she put him off one time too many? Had he found someone else in these long months apart? Had he come to care for Mary Upton?

The decision that could change her life forever had come in the quiet of the night, while she'd been praying. Suddenly she knew: If she had to make a choice between opera and Steve, it would be Steve. The intensity of desire that had been part of her very soul, and had driven her toward her career since she'd been twelve years old, was gone, replaced by a new desire, to love the Reverend Steve Shepherd, and share his ministry.

What had made her know that was the right decision was a rock solid acceptance that she didn't really care whether her voice returned fully or not. She knew her course, and it was south, to Georgia, to a man like no other she had ever known, to a man God had chosen for her, she was sure.

Oh, please, dear Lord, Serena prayed now, *let there be*

a shred of caring in his heart.

Another reason she had waited so long to come to him was that she prayed her voice would heal completely so he would know she was not choosing him because her career was over, and she was settling for second best. Oh no, she had to convince him she wanted *him* more than anything else in life. If her voice had not healed, the convincing might have been more difficult, but she would have found a way, somehow, to persuade him they belonged together.

"You know why I've come, don't you?" she said to Miss Vivian, who had not stopped smiling since she'd picked Serena up at the airport.

"I thought you would, sooner or later."

Serena gave her an affectionate look. "How could you know that?"

"Because if ever I saw two people in love, it was you and Stephen." She grinned. "And I helped."

Serena shook her head back and forth in amazement. "You mean all the time I was staying with you, and thought you were sweet and innocent, and really did have a headache so that you couldn't be with us, you were actually playing matchmaker?"

"To the best of my ability."

Serena reached over and squeezed Miss Vivian's hand on the steering wheel. "Thank you, my dear friend. Now if your marvelous pastor will only cooperate."

"And ask you to marry him?"

"No, just say yes when *I* ask *him* to marry me."

Miss Vivian squealed in delight. "I'd like to see the look on his face when you do that."

"Don't think I won't, Miss Vivian. This is the nineties, you know. Women speak up for what they want."

Vivian became serious. "I know you love Stephen, Serena, but what about your career? You can't keep that up and be a pastor's wife, too."

"I don't intend to. I've given up my career, even though I'm perfectly able to resume it. God has shown me that Steve, and our life together, are more important."

For a fleeting second doubt loomed in her thoughts. "He will want me, won't he, Miss Vivian?"

Vivian gave her an adoring look. "Oh, yes, Serena, he will want you. Stephen is a most intelligent man, and will surely recognize that you are the best thing that's ever happened to him. . .after his relationship with God, of course."

Serena felt completely at home when they got to Miss Vivian's, and filled with energy, went off to prepare herself for the most important conversation she would ever have.

She showered, repaired her makeup, and changed clothes, putting on an outfit Steve had seen her in once and had admired—a slim, olive green corduroy skirt and matching cotton blouse, with a fragile gold necklace of two strands draped around its neck. Large gold loop earrings completed her jewelry. She wore her hair down, fluffed at her shoulders.

Do I need a sweater? she asked herself. *No, it's not that cold, and I'm going to be indoors.*

Checking her image one last time in the bathroom mirror, Serena dabbed her favorite perfume behind her ears, at her throat, and on her wrists.

Her stomach was in knots. She had never asked a man to marry her before, and had no idea in the world how to do so, but she was determined to do it, even knowing there was a chance Steve would turn her down.

twenty-two

At the church, a regular work day was in process. She met Randall Dawson going into the choir room, a stack of cantata books in his chubby arms.

"Serena," he exclaimed, "it's wonderful to see you again." He dropped the books on the nearest table, turned, and grabbed both her hands in his. "How is your throat?"

"Good as new. Thanks for asking."

"You look. . .beautiful." His eyes swept quickly over her. "How long will you be in town?"

Serena's pulse quickened. "I'm not sure. How are things going with the new music school you've started here at the church?"

"Great, thanks to your underwriting it. Between instruments and music, it hasn't been cheap."

"A small enough return to God for all He's given me."

"We have twenty-three kids enrolled, you know, and I couldn't be more pleased with the results. All of our teachers are volunteers. It's amazing how much musical talent there is in a church when you go hunting for it. We're offering instruction in brass, winds, strings, percussion, vocal, piano, and organ. It's exciting."

"You've accomplished a lot in a short time, Randall. The reports you've sent me are thorough and encouraging."

"Your generosity is making a musical education possible for a lot of deserving kids who, we hope, will use that music in the church. You should be commended publicly so people will know what you are doing."

"I don't want any praise, Randall," Serena said.

"I know you don't, that's part of what makes you so wonderful."

Serena blushed and murmured, "I have to be going. See you Sunday."

"Would you sing a solo for us? Anything you want."

Serena didn't pause to think about it. "Sure. I've just put music to some words from several of the Psalms. It's called 'A New Song.' Will you play for me?" Randall was an outstanding accompanist.

"I'd be honored. When do you want to practice?"

"I'll call you."

"Okay."

Serena hurried off, anxious to see Steve, intent on honestly sharing her feelings with him, no matter what his reaction. Nothing gained, nothing ventured, her dad always used to say.

Sally Griffin was at her desk and jumped up when Serena came into the church office.

"Miss Lawrence, how wonderful to see you again. How are you?"

Serena grasped her hands. "Just fine, Sally. How are you?"

"Nervous. I'm getting married in three weeks."

"Really? Well, congratulations." They hugged each other. "Is he someone I know?"

"Roger Dunbar. He sings in the choir, and teaches violin in the church's new music school. He also instructs at the local college."

"I'm happy for you," Serena told her.

"How is your voice, Miss Lawrence?"

"It's fully recovered, Sally, and please call me Serena."

Sally murmured agreement.

"It took awhile, but I guess the Lord thought I needed to learn patience, and He's been with me all the way."

"Of course He was. Didn't He say, 'I will never leave you nor forsake you'?"

"That He did."

The door to Steve's office opened with a jerk. "Serena! What are you doing here?" The astonished, but pleased, look on his face when he saw her gave Serena courage.

She walked toward him. "I have something to ask you, Stephen Shepherd," and he closed the door behind them when she entered his office.

The room looked the same as she had remembered it from months before—still welcoming yet meant for business, still speaking of the open and friendly personality of its occupant.

Her heart raced wildly now. Finally, after all the thinking and planning, she was in the same room with him. Would she have the courage to do what she'd come to do?

She wanted to fly into his arms, and she hoped he wanted her to, but there was an awkwardness between them, caused by months of separation.

She walked slowly through the room, her eyes taking in every book and piece of furniture. The words she had rehearsed so many times were muddled in her brain, and she felt like running.

She stopped in front of the bookcase and picked up a music box. Turning the key on the bottom, she listened with interest as it played a pretty tune.

Steve came up behind her. She could feel the warmth from his tall body. "It's from one of the students at our new music school. He gave it to me in thanks for being able to take lessons here."

He turned her around with the same strong hands she remembered, and gazed deep into her eyes. "Serena, yours was a good idea—to teach music here at the church."

She smiled, happy that he now thought so.

"We appreciate more than we can say your funding of it, too. I hope it isn't a burden."

"It's not, believe me."

He dropped his hands, and almost looked shy. "Why are you here, Serena? I never expected you—I wrote you—"

"Letters I did not answer as promptly as I should have, if at all," she answered guiltily. "I'm sorry."

"I called as well, and left messages on your answer phone—"

"Which I returned."

He frowned. "Eventually, yes." There was no smile on his face now, or joy in his intense brown eyes, only questions, and Serena's determination to boldly express her feelings wavered.

"I. . .I came. . .I've missed you," she said, knowing he would find that hard to believe after she'd been so uncommunicative.

"Really? The last time we saw each other, when I was in New York, I thought we meant something to each other. But then you made it clear to me you no longer wanted me in your life."

"Oh, Steve, that's not true." Her heart lifted. "I know I should have contacted you more, but I've had a lot to think about these past few months."

"Seven months, Serena."

He was not going to make this easy for her. "Yes, seven months."

His expression softened a little. "How is your throat?

Tell me what the doctor says."

She smiled. "He's done all he can. It has healed beyond his expectations."

"Thank God."

"Oh, I do thank Him, every single day."

"You can go on with your career now?"

"Yes, but—"

"I'm happy for you, Serena. That's what you want more than anything—to sing with that glorious voice. The world will be happy to have you back."

She knew he meant the words, but they lacked enthusiasm, as did the expression in his eyes that told her he thought she would be lost to him forever now.

"Oh, Steve," she took his arm and pulled him over to a couch where they both sat down and faced each other, "I've drawn so much closer to God during this time. I've learned to pray, not just asking Him for healing, but thanking Him for whatever lesson I should be learning in this trouble. I've read His Scriptures and have gained a real peace, which He promised so many times."

Steve's bushy eyebrows raised in question. "So you were able to face the possibility of your voice never returning to what it was?"

"Yes, I was."

"That takes courage and faith."

"I'm still learning."

She shifted her position on the couch, knowing that it was now or never. "Steve, I've made a major decision. I don't want an opera career anymore."

Steve's mouth gaped open. "Serena, what are you saying?"

She leaned over and took his precious face between her two hands. Then she leaned forward and kissed him gently on the lips.

"I'm saying that I want to do something else with my life."

"Something else?"

A slow smile grew across her mouth. "I want to get married."

"What?"

"Stephen Shepherd, will you marry me?"

Steve just sat there, stunned.

Serena rushed on. "I want to marry you, Steve. You know I love you. I admire and respect you and your work. I'm wholly committed to the Lord, to do His will, and I believe His will for me is to be here in this church, with you, teaching music—"

Steve grabbed her arms. "Wait. You're not serious."

"Yes, I am, Steve. I've been thinking about it for months now, what it would be like to be married to you—"

"Serena, you don't know what you're saying."

"Yes, I do." She put her arms around his waist and snuggled against his shoulder. "It will be wonderful, darling, you'll see. We are meant for each other. I'm sure God brought us together."

Steve gently pushed her away and rose to his feet, his face wreathed in doubt while he stared at her. "Serena, this makes no sense. You're a star. Your voice has healed. You can resume your career. Do you honestly think you could be happy, instead, living in a small town, married to. . .to. . . ."

"The most wonderful man in the world?" Serena jumped up and faced him. "Yes, oh, yes. Of course I would be happy."

"For a time, perhaps, but then you would start to miss the glamorous life you're a part of now. I could never give you the money, the prestige—"

Serena placed two fingers over his mouth. "What you *can* give me is the kind of love every woman desires— faithful, enduring, exciting."

Steve backed away from her. "No, Serena, you're dreaming. In time you would become bored and long for your former life. It just won't work."

twenty-three

"Steve," Serena hurried on, more convinced than ever that she could make him understand why she had just proposed to him, "I know you're worried that when you marry again the same thing will happen as did with Stacia, that you'll spend too much time apart for the sake of your ministry, and it will undermine the marriage. But I believe part of that problem stemmed from her unwillingness to share you with those whom you are called to serve. I understand that calling. I know I must share you, but I feel called too, not just to be your wife, but to minister to the people in my own way."

Steve stared at her; he wanted to believe her, but he couldn't. This was not just any woman talking to him, it was Serena Lawrence, brilliant megastar. To confine her to an ordinary existence would be like caging a treasure that belonged to everyone. He couldn't do that, and he was sure she did not really understand what she was suggesting. She did not know what a totally different pace of life the people of this area lived compared with what she was used to.

He stared into her gorgeous jade eyes, so filled with love that he knew could not last. "Serena, you flatter me beyond words with your. . . ."

"Proposal," she reminded him.

"Dream," he insisted, taking one of her hands and holding it, caressing the back of it, then lifting it to his lips and keeping it there. He shut his eyes, facing the agonizing temptation to just say yes to her, take a wild, unprincipled chance and marry her, and keep her all for himself for as long as he could, knowing she would leave him sooner or later.

He could almost physically hear Satan saying in his ear, "You're the luckiest of men, Shepherd, to have Serena Lawrence want you. Go on, marry her, enjoy a time of love. Who knows, it just might work."

"No, it won't work," he answered the Tempter out loud, and Serena's expression changed from one of adoration to one of alarm.

"Don't give up on us until you've had a chance to think about it, Steve. I know my return to fellowship with the Lord is new and untried. I'll understand if you want to wait six months or a year to marry, to be sure it's genuine, and to be sure my decision about my career is what I truly want. I'll wait for you."

Steve's knees weakened. When she looked at him like that, all compliance and love and promising a togetherness he had dreamed of, he could barely retain his rationality.

He was a man, after all, able to be tempted, longing for love and fulfillment just like any other man. Why not take a chance? Maybe she was right, maybe God had brought them together. He had fallen in love with her so easily, but he could not imagine her returning those feelings. And yet here she was, with her outrageous proposal.

Oh, God, what do I do? he prayed. *What is the right thing to do, for both of us?*

She started to kiss him.

"Serena, don't. . . please, we have to be realistic about this. Serena. . . ."

She wrapped her arms around his neck and played with his hair until he pulled her into his arms and kissed her hungrily, marveling that such an exquisite creation of God could actually love him and want to serve with him in his ministry.

Her lips blended excitingly with his, and she murmured his name in a soft, enchanting voice. He kept on holding her even though he knew he must convince her that they could not marry. He didn't know what to say, though, not when that was what he wanted more than anything else in the world.

The door to his office burst open, and his secretary rushed in, ignoring them, and turned on the small television that sat on a bookcase shelf. "Pastor, you must hear this. A tornado warning for Hall County has just been issued."

The voice of an announcer filled the room as Serena and Steve separated and gave their attention to what was being broadcast.

"From the 11 Alive Weather Watch Office. The National Weather Service in Athens has issued a tornado warning effective until 3:15 Eastern Daylight time for people in the following locations. . . ."

They watched the screen and Serena gasped when she saw Hall County listed. She had been through earthquakes and floods, but never a tornado. The thought of it frightened her beyond words.

Steve went to the garden door and jerked it open, stepping outside, where he looked up and cocked his head, as though listening for something.

Serena followed, suddenly needing a breath of the cool, fresh air. To her amazement, the air was now still, warm, and humid. *How strange that it changed so suddenly*, she thought.

"It's coming," Steve announced, his brow plunging to a deep frown, and Serena heard in the distance a low roar, like the sound of an approaching freight train.

"Quick, Serena, get inside."

With his strong hand on her waist, Steve literally pushed her back into the building. "Sally," he spoke firmly to his secretary, "we have to get everyone in the storm cellar. Now!"

Bursting out of his office, the three of them ran along the corridor, Steve and Sally yelling into every room they passed, warning anyone inside of the impending danger. A half-dozen people joined them, including Randall Dawson. "I already checked the sanctuary; no one's in it," he reported to Steve.

"Good."

By the time they reached a door marked EMERGENCY, they could feel the vibration of the violent wind and hear the crashing of trees and other objects pummeling the church. Serena feared they were all going to die.

Steve yanked the door open and waited for the others to go before him down a flight of well-lit stairs. Serena wanted to wait for him, to be sure he was with them. When she turned around, though, she almost fell down the stairs. Randall caught her and said, "Keep moving. He'll be all right."

Her heart pounded against her rib cage and she prayed, "Oh, Lord, please protect these Your people and this church."

Now it sounded as though a dozen trains were all converging just beyond the wall, and the roar grew more deafening as Serena and the others dashed down the stairs and into a fifty-by-fifty cement-walled room that was filled with mattresses, chairs, sofas, tables and cabinets.

Steve was beside her, helping her and the other women down on the floor after which he covered each of them with a mattress.

"Stay there and don't move," he commanded, and Serena

did not question as she heard anxious voices all around her invoking the name of God in prayer. Would the solid cement walls be enough protection from the violence of the storm?

As she lay there, trembling, she listened frantically for Steve's voice, knowing he was still on his feet, helping others to protect themselves regardless of the danger to himself.

Because of the many mattresses, she figured the ceiling of the room was not cement, as were the walls. The tornado could very likely lift the entire church off its foundation and suck them all into oblivion.

She had never before been so frightened until she remembered the verse, "Yea, though I walk through the valley of the shadow of death, I will fear no evil, for Thou art with me." She knew God was with them, there in that shelter. In fully realizing that, a surge of peace came upon her; her heart stilled and her hands, which had been clenched in painful fists, relaxed.

Then the tornado struck the building. The lights went out and people screamed. Serena heard the final deadly roar, and then the silence. The incredible silence.

twenty-four

The church was not destroyed, but one entire corner of it was lifted off and carried away to no one knew where. Trees, ripped from the ground by their roots, lay everywhere like discarded match sticks. Power lines were down, roads blocked.

A brand new 4x4 pickup was sitting on the steps to the front door of the church, squashed to the ground as though a giant had carelessly stepped on it. A delicate ceramic table lamp sat on the brick steps beside it, undamaged.

People moaned and cried for help, some of them injured and bleeding, others disoriented.

Serena rushed into Steve's arms when it was over, thanking God that he was all right, as were all the others who had been in the storm cellar with them. "Are you okay?" he questioned her anxiously.

When she said, "I'm fine, really," he hugged her fiercely, then let her go. There was work to be done.

He and Serena worked side by side, comforting people, reuniting families, administering first aid until the paramedics and ambulances arrived, giving out bottled water that had been stored in the church's storm cellar.

Steve remembered the accounts of the tornado of 1936, where over 200 people were killed, 1,000 injured, and nearly 800 homes and most of downtown Graylin had been destroyed. He prayed this twister had not been as severe, but it looked bad.

His office was gone, as was a third of the beautiful stained-glass sanctuary. Glass was everywhere.

The massive destruction was offset by moments of

wonder, as he spotted a canceled check on the ground, picked it up, and saw that it was from a bank in a town eighty miles away. The check was wet, but clean and legible.

Three nearby buildings were leveled. Others, across the street, were untouched, demonstrating the inexplicable random destruction of the storm.

Hours later, tired, disheveled, his suit torn and filthy, Steve found Serena sitting on a patch of grass beneath a tree that had lost half its branches. She was as dirty as he was and shivering, one sleeve of her cotton blouse torn nearly from its shoulder, but she looked like an angel, holding a small child in her arms, feeding him a cup of water.

"Hi, there." Steve took off his jacket and put it around her shoulders. She looked up at him with sad and tired eyes but managed a wan smile. Squatting down beside her, he gently ruffled the hair of the little boy who was a stranger to him, and asked, "Y'all okay?"

The child burrowed deeper into Serena's embrace and wouldn't answer, but Serena said, "We're fine." Tears rolled down her cheeks. "This is terrible. I've never been through anything like it."

"I'm sorry."

"It makes one appreciate every day we're given, and how careful we should be to make the most of it."

Steve nodded.

"I'm s. . .so glad you're all r. . .right," she stammered, and he knew she was trying not to cry in front of the child, but desperately needed to.

He winked at her then and grinned, for the first time in many hours. "I have to be all right," he said. "I'm getting married."

Her eyes lit up just before he kissed her lightly.

The tornado's destruction was widespread, racing over three counties, but no deaths were reported, and the towns and cities of northeast Georgia began rebuilding.

Serena felt awful about the destruction to Steve's church, and when they were having dinner together the next night, at Victor's, the same restaurant Steve had taken her to when she'd first arrived in town, she held his hand across the candlelit table and said, "We both have rebuilding to do, don't we—my life and your church? Let's do it together."

Steve still thought he was living another man's life, to have Serena Lawrence wanting to marry him, but here she was, eye-pleasing in a sophisticated vee-necked dress of rust-colored wool, her gold jewelry catching the candlelight, her hand so soft and warm in his.

"Together is the operative word. I accept your proposal of marriage."

"Oh, Steve." Serena jumped up and came to him, throwing her arms around his neck as he struggled to get up and return her hug. They kissed, not even realizing several people were watching them and smiling at their exuberant display of affection.

"You won't change your mind, will you?" he asked, as they both resumed their seats, their eyes fastened on each other.

"Absolutely not," Serena declared.

"I *have* told you today how much I love you, haven't I?"

"Today, tonight, and only five minutes ago," Serena murmured.

"Good. So, when shall we be married?"

Serena toyed with the shrimp scampi on her plate for a moment with her fork, then gazed into Steve's eyes and said, "I think we should wait a year."

He let out a rush of air. "Too long."

"I mentioned this before," she said, "in your office. I want you to be sure my recommitment to the Lord is solid, and my giving up my career is really what I want to do. You must have no doubts as to whether either will be lasting."

"Serena, no—"

"Please, Steve, it's important to give ourselves time, for you and the people of your congregation to be sure of me. I wouldn't want to disappoint you." She grinned. "Make no mistake, though, I am not going to let you get away."

"You'd better not."

Steve was stunned with her spiritual insight and knew, indeed, it would be wise to test her new resolves. It would be hard to wait, though. He loved her so much, and wanted to be with her every minute. He wanted the intimacy of a married relationship with her, not just the physical part but the emotional and spiritual as well. That's what he wanted, but her wisdom should be respected, so he agreed.

"I would wait for you forever, Serena," he vowed.

"And I for you."

They held hands and saw the love in each other's eyes and knew God had worked a mysterious miracle in bringing them together, for which they would praise Him for the rest of their lives.

The following Sunday Serena sang a hauntingly beautiful song in the morning service, where a sunny breeze drifted into the sanctuary through the torn-away roof. A tiny bird accompanied her from a hiding place in the rafters. Randall played the piano for her, and there was hardly a dry eye in the congregation when she sang the simple song with words from Psalm 144: "I will sing a new song to You, O God. Happy are the people whose God is the Lord!"

epilogue

"October is such a beautiful month, don't you think?" Serena asked Steve, as she lay in his arms in the soft double bed, relishing the quiet morning moments. The windows of their bedroom were open and a few feisty birds were chattering to each other as the sun moved beyond the horizon and into the cloudless sky.

"It's the best month of the year," Steve agreed, kissing her forehead. "We got married just one year ago, in October."

"Yes, and now we have twins, Andrew Stephen and Elizabeth Dawn, born in October." She snuggled against Steve, her hand light on his chest. "I can't believe they're both quiet at the same time. Am I dreaming?"

A low murmur of satisfaction rose from Steve's throat and his arms tightened around her. "I started dreaming the night I first saw you, Serena Lawrence Shepherd, and I haven't stopped since. Hasn't God blessed us beyond belief?"

"Oh, yes, He has. We found each other and fell in love. My throat had no cancer and completely healed. Rebuilding the church after the tornado united our people in sweet Christian togetherness, and then we married the next year, and here we are, another year later, with a son and daughter, both healthy and wonderful."

Deep emotion and tears in his eyes kept Steve from replying, but Serena felt the warmth of his arms around her and knew he shared her awe at what had happened in their lives.

"I love you, Steve Shepherd."

"And I, you, Serena."

Two piercing infant cries split the air, and Andrew and Elizabeth's parents giggled, then groaned as they dragged themselves out of bed.

"It's your turn to change the diapers," Serena said, pulling on her apricot terry robe.

Steve shook his head no. "I did them last night, Mom. It's your turn."

"If you do the diapers, I'll start the coffee."

"*I'll* do the coffee and *you* do the diapers."

The baby screams heightened and both harried parents gazed at each other, shrugged, then with arms around each other's waist, trudged down the hall to the nursery, ready if not quite eager, to attend to the needs of their impatient family.

Steve gazed at Serena and marveled at how beautiful she was, even after thirty years. Her thick auburn hair had only a trace of gray, and he still loved to roam his fingers through it. Her deep-set eyes of jade had never lost their sparkle, and her skin was still soft to the touch.

How often I have kissed that pert, upturned nose, he thought with a rush of gratitude for the many years he'd been blessed to spend with her. *How often I have kissed that mouth that smiles just for me.*

She still held incredible appeal to him, the years enhancing their relationship, bringing them closer as they got to know each other in every facet of their personalities. Not that she didn't have a fault or two, or they hadn't had their share of disagreements, but he still held her in awe, as he had the exquisite opera diva he had first seen on a concert stage in Atlanta. Then, she had owned the heart of the world; since, she had owned *his* heart, and that of every person in their church, as well as those of their children.

She turned to him with barely contained excitement. "Oh, Steve, can you believe it? Our Elizabeth is about to make her debut at the Met."

"Singing the role in *Madama Butterfly* that made her incomparable mother famous a few years ago."

Serena squeezed his hands and tiny lines crinkled around her lovely eyes. "A few years, yes."

"Then tomorrow we hear Andrew preach his first sermon at his new church."

"We are blessed with two marvelous children who give us nearly constant joy," Serena agreed with a broad smile. Then her eyes darkened, "And our third child is one step away from jail."

Steve frowned, thinking of Scott—headstrong, stubborn, never accepting the Lord, and having no idea what he wanted to do with his life. He was nineteen, and a dropout from college.

"I know our story is not unique," Serena went on. "There are Christian parents everywhere who have one special child they cannot reach. No matter how much one loves and nurtures, and guides with God's help, we cannot *make* our children happy and accepting of God's salvation."

"To be truthful," Steve said reflectively, "my heart has always belonged to Scott more than Elizabeth and Andrew."

"Because he has always needed us more."

"But wanted us less," Steve grunted.

The door to the dressing room swept open, and there she was, their darling Elizabeth, in her Japanese kimono and wig, her waist bound in an obi and her feet in small canvas shoes, looking like a stranger in her dark hair and Oriental makeup. They both rose from the sofa on which they'd been sitting and went to her, carefully hugging so as not to disturb her attire.

"We are so very proud of you," Steve said, a lump

rising in his throat. Hadn't it been only yesterday when they'd brought her home from the hospital, all pink and new, and staring up at him as though asking who he was to be in her life.

"You will be a most beautiful Cio-Cio-San," Serena enthused, thrilled for the success of her darling daughter, more thrilled because she, too, was a Christian.

"Not more than my incomparable mother," Elizabeth insisted. "You are still a legend in the world of opera, you know, Mom."

"Am I really?"

"Yes."

They left her and went out front to their seats. Andrew was there, all six-feet-three of him, with dark curly hair and sparkling blue eyes. He was a charmer, complete with his father's dimples, but he was a good, decent man who had known from childhood that he wanted to be in the ministry.

"How's the kid?" he asked, giving Serena a kiss on the cheek. "Nervous? Ready to faint? No, she'll be great. She has your talent, Mom, and your courage, Dad. Oh, there's someone I have to see. Excuse me a minute, please."

Serena and Steve watched their strapping son move into the crowd and greet a stunning blonde girl who looked up at him adoringly.

"Uh oh," Steve said. "Do I hear wedding bells?"

Serena turned and smiled at this remarkable man who had been her devoted husband for so many years, and whom she loved even more passionately now than she had the day they married.

Their lives had been rich in countless ways, and she had never regretted giving up her career to marry him. The years had been filled with helping young people discover their music abilities, being on the Board of Directors of the Arts

Council, and in being "the pastor's wife," a title she relished and worked hard to fulfill in every way that was pleasing to God, then to Steve.

Thank goodness I followed the leading of the Lord, she thought, gazing at her beloved husband, or I would never have known the bliss of our lives together. She praised God silently for the new song He had given her, which had lasted a lifetime, and would greet her in eternity.

"I love you," she whispered to Steve, as the orchestra began to play.

"No more than I love you," he answered, kissing her fingertips.

The curtain rose, and the music went on.

A Letter To Our Readers

Dear Reader:

In order that we might better contribute to your reading enjoyment, we would appreciate your taking a few minutes to respond to the following questions. When completed, please return to the following:

Rebecca Germany, Editor
Heartsong Presents
P.O. Box 719
Uhrichsville, Ohio 44683

1. Did you enjoy reading *A New Song*?
   ☐ Very much. I would like to see more books
     by this author!
   ☐ Moderately
     I would have enjoyed it more if _____

   _____

2. Are you a member of *Heartsong Presents*? Yes   No
   If no, where did you purchase this book? _____

   _____

3. What influenced your decision to purchase
   this book? (Circle those that apply.)

   Cover   Back cover copy

   Title   Friends

   Publicity   Other _____

4. On a scale from 1 (poor) to 10 (superior), please rate the following elements.

___Heroine   ___Plot

___Hero   ___Inspirational theme

___Setting   ___Secondary characters

5. What settings would you like to see covered in *Heartsong Presents* books?

_____

_____

6. What are some inspirational themes you would like to see treated in future books?_____

_____

_____

7. Would you be interested in reading other *Heartsong Presents* titles?   Yes   No

8. Please circle your age range:
   Under 18   18-24   25-34
   35-45   46-55   Over 55

9. How many hours per week do you read? _____

Name _____

Occupation _____

Address _____

City _____ State _____ Zip _____

Coming Soon!

From *Heartsong Presents*

A New Contemporary Romance by
Rena Eastman

Midsummer's Dream (HP73)

Suffocated by her life, Salisa Vrendren embarks on a mission.

Hopefully, a year as a Christian Union representative at Abingdon University in Abingdon, England, will help Salisa know what God wants her to do.

But Salisa still has her doubts. Should she return to Michigan and accept Dale's proposal of marriage? Or is Nigel Worthington, a fellow Christian Union rep, the man God wants her to marry? Even though Nigel is British, a life with him wouldn't be too different from one with Dale. Then there is the charming medical student, Bennett Havana, who seems to know her as only a true heartmate could.

Is Salisa's future to be only a midsummer's dream, founded in fantasy, or a real, down-to-earth romance secured by a deep faith?

····· Hearts♥ng ·········

ROMANCE IS CHEAPER BY THE DOZEN!

Any 12 *Heartsong Presents* titles for only $26.95 *

Buy any assortment of twelve *Heartsong Presents* titles and save 25% off of the already discounted price of $2.95 each!

plus $1.00 shipping and handling per order and sales tax where applicable.

HEARTSONG PRESENTS TITLES AVAILABLE NOW:

__HP 1 A TORCH FOR TRINITY, *Colleen L. Reece*
__HP 2 WILDFLOWER HARVEST, *Colleen L. Reece*
__HP 3 RESTORE THE JOY, *Sara Mitchell*
__HP 4 REFLECTIONS OF THE HEART, *Sally Laity*
__HP 5 THIS TREMBLING CUP, *Marlene Chase*
__HP 6 THE OTHER SIDE OF SILENCE, *Marlene Chase*
__HP 7 CANDLESHINE, *Colleen L. Reece*
__HP 8 DESERT ROSE, *Colleen L. Reece*
__HP 9 HEARTSTRINGS, *Irene B. Brand*
__HP10 SONG OF LAUGHTER, *Lauraine Snelling*
__HP11 RIVER OF FIRE, *Jacquelyn Cook*
__HP13 PASSAGE OF THE HEART, *Kjersti Hoff Baez*
__HP14 A MATTER OF CHOICE, *Susannah Hayden*
__HP15 WHISPERS ON THE WIND, *Maryn Langer*
__HP16 SILENCE IN THE SAGE, *Colleen L. Reece*
__HP17 LLAMA LADY, *VeraLee Wiggins*
__HP18 ESCORT HOMEWARD, *Eileen M. Berger*
__HP19 A PLACE TO BELONG, *Janelle Jamison*
__HP20 SHORES OF PROMISE, *Kate Blackwell*
__HP21 GENTLE PERSUASION, *Veda Boyd Jones*
__HP22 INDY GIRL, *Brenda Bancroft*
__HP23 GONE WEST, *Kathleen Karr*
__HP24 WHISPERS IN THE WILDERNESS, *Colleen L. Reece*
__HP25 REBAR, *Mary Carpenter Reid*
__HP26 MOUNTAIN HOUSE, *Mary Louise Colln*
__HP27 BEYOND THE SEARCHING RIVER, *Jacquelyn Cook*
__HP28 DAKOTA DAWN, *Lauraine Snelling*
__HP29 FROM THE HEART, *Sara Mitchell*
__HP30 A LOVE MEANT TO BE, *Brenda Bancroft*
__HP31 DREAM SPINNER, *Sally Laity*
__HP32 THE PROMISED LAND, *Kathleen Karr*
__HP33 SWEET SHELTER, *VeraLee Wiggins*
__HP34 UNDER A TEXAS SKY, *Veda Boyd Jones*
__HP35 WHEN COMES THE DAWN, *Brenda Bancroft*
__HP36 THE SURE PROMISE, *JoAnn A. Grote*
__HP37 DRUMS OF SHELOMOH, *Yvonne Lehman*
__HP38 A PLACE TO CALL HOME, *Eileen M. Berger*
__HP39 RAINBOW HARVEST, *Norene Morris*
__HP40 PERFECT LOVE, *Janelle Jamison*
__HP41 FIELDS OF SWEET CONTENT, *Norma Jean Lutz*
__HP42 SEARCH FOR TOMORROW, *Mary Hawkins*

(If ordering from this page, please remember to include it with the order form.)

·········· Presents ··········

_HP43 VEILED JOY, *Colleen L. Reece*
_HP44 DAKOTA DREAM, *Lauraine Snelling*
_HP45 DESIGN FOR LOVE, *Janet Gortsema*
_HP46 THE GOVERNOR'S DAUGHTER, *Veda Boyd Jones*
_HP47 TENDER JOURNEYS, *Janelle Jamison*
_HP48 SHORES OF DELIVERANCE, *Kate Blackwell*
_HP49 YESTERDAY'S TOMORROWS, *Linda Herring*
_HP50 DANCE IN THE DISTANCE, *Kjersti Hoff Baez*
_HP51 THE UNFOLDING HEART, *JoAnn A. Grote*
_HP52 TAPESTRY OF TAMAR, *Colleen L. Reece*
_HP53 MIDNIGHT MUSIC, *Janelle Burnham*
_HP54 HOME TO HER HEART, *Lena Nelson Dooley*
_HP55 TREASURE OF THE HEART, *JoAnn A. Grote*
_HP56 A LIGHT IN THE WINDOW, *Janelle Jamison*
_HP57 LOVE'S SILKEN MELODY, *Norma Jean Lutz*
_HP58 FREE TO LOVE, *Doris English*
_HP59 EYES OF THE HEART, *Maryn Langer*
_HP60 MORE THAN CONQUERORS, *Kay Cornelius*
_HP61 PICTURE PERFECT, *Susan Kirby*
_HP62 A REAL AND PRECIOUS THING, *Brenda Bancroft*
_HP63 THE WILLING HEART, *Janelle Jamison*
_HP65 CROWS'-NESTS AND MIRRORS, *Colleen L. Reece*
_HP66 ANGEL FACE, *Frances Carfi Matranga*
_HP67 AUTUMN LOVE, *Ann Bell*
_HP68 DAKOTA DUSK, *Lauraine Snelling*
_HP69 RIVERS RUSHING TO THE SEA, *Jacquelyn Cook*
_HP70 BETWEEN LOVE AND LOYALTY, *Susannah Hayden*
_HP71 A NEW SONG, *Kathleen Yapp*
_HP72 DESTINEY'S ROAD, *Janelle Jamison*
_HP73 SONG OF CAPTIVITY, *Linda Herring*

Great Inspirational Romance at a Great Price!

Heartsong Presents books are inspirational romances in contemporary and historical settings, designed to give you an enjoyable, spirit-lifting reading experience. You can choose from 73 wonderfully written titles from some of today's best authors like Colleen L. Reece, Brenda Bancroft, Janelle Jamison, and many others.

When ordering quantities less than twelve, above titles are $2.95 each.

SEND TO: Heartsong Presents Reader's Service
P.O. Box 719, Uhrichsville, Ohio 44683

Please send me the items checked above. I am enclosing $_____
(please add $1.00 to cover postage per order. OH add 6.5% tax. PA and NJ add 6%.). Send check or money order, no cash or C.O.D.s, please.
To place a credit card order, call 1-800-847-8270.

NAME _____

ADDRESS _____

CITY/STATE _____ ZIP _____

HPS APRIL

LOVE A GREAT LOVE STORY?

Introducing Heartsong Presents —
                    Your Inspirational Book Club

   Heartsong Presents Christian romance reader's service will provide you with four never before published romance titles every month! In fact, your books will be mailed to you at the same time advance copies are sent to book reviewers. You'll preview each of these new and unabridged books before they are released to the general public.

   These books are filled with the kind of stories you have been longing for—stories of courtship, chivalry, honor, and virtue. Strong characters and riveting plot lines will make you want to read on and on. Romance is not dead, and each of these romantic tales will remind you that Christian faith is still the vital ingredient in an intimate relationship filled with true love and honest devotion.

   Sign up today to receive your first set. Send no money now. We'll bill you only $9.97 post-paid with your shipment. Then every month you'll automatically receive the latest four "hot off the press" titles for the same low post-paid price of $9.97. That's a savings of 50% off the $4.95 cover price. When you consider the exaggerated shipping charges of other book clubs, your savings are even greater!

   THERE IS NO RISK—you may cancel at any time without obligation. And if you aren't completely satisfied with any selection, return it for an immediate refund.

   TO JOIN, just complete the coupon below, mail it today, and get ready for hours of wholesome entertainment.

   Now you can curl up, relax, and enjoy some great reading full of the warmhearted spirit of romance.

┌ ─ ─ ─ ─ ─ Curl up with Heartsong! ─ ─ ─ ─ ┐

YES! Sign me up for Heartsong!

NEW MEMBERSHIPS WILL BE SHIPPED IMMEDIATELY!
Send no money now. We'll bill you only $9.97 post-paid with your first shipment of four books. Or for faster action, call toll free 1-800-847-8270.

NAME_____

ADDRESS_____

CITY_____ STATE / ZIP _____
  MAIL TO: HEARTSONG / P.O. Box 719 Uhrichsville, Ohio 44683
YES II